ALSO BY JEFFREY FRANK

The Columnist

BAD PUBLICITY

A NOVEL

JEFFREY FRANK

SIMON & SCHUSTER

NEW YORK LONDON TORONTO SYDNEY SINGAPORE

SIMON & SCHUSTER
Rockefeller Center
1230 Avenue of the Americas
New York, NY 10020

SIMON & SCHUSTER and colophon are registered trademarks
of Simon & Schuster, Inc.

For information regarding special discounts for bulk purchases,
please contact Simon & Schuster Special Sales at 1-800-456-6798
or business@simonandschuster.com

Manufactured in the United States of America

1   3   5   7   9   10   8   6   4   2

Library of Congress Cataloging-in-Publication Data
Frank, Jeffrey.
Bad publicity : a novel / Jeffrey Frank.
p.   cm.
I. Title.
PS3556.R33423B33   2004   813'.54—dc22   2003057342
ISBN 0-7432-4776-0

IN MEMORY OF MY PARENTS

BAD
PUBLICITY

ONE

By September of 1987 Charles Dingleman had become the sort of person who muttered obscenities when the supermarket line moved too slowly. He complained so often about so many little things that people in his law firm rolled their eyes and his young second wife said that he had become tiresome. Charlie, as everyone called him, had not been the same since he'd lost his seat in Congress three years before. He could still be charming, especially when he wore his wide smile and sincere stare, and he liked to tell clients that serving six years as the servant of a half-million Pennsylvanians was his proudest accomplishment. But no one quite believed him, perhaps because Charlie could not entirely conceal the loathing he felt for the tens of thousands of people who'd voted against him, and he never seemed comfortable talking about that time of his life.

The truth was that the people of Pennsylvania had turned on Charlie, and they had their reasons: a public divorce, which not only left him feeling sorry at the way everything had turned out but ashamed of himself. "I just kept stepping into it," he liked to say, but then he somehow did it again.

Just that week he'd managed to offend one of the associates, a dark-haired thirty-year-old named Judith Grust, who had been on the *Law Review* at Harvard and was often at the office past midnight, working much harder than Charlie ever would. On an impulse that

Charlie thought was genuine (twice she'd smiled at him in the corridor), he'd invited Judith to lunch to discuss a mineral rights case that she'd helped him to prepare, producing a brief so intelligent and so detailed that he found it hard to follow. It was a lawsuit of very little interest to Charlie, and he found himself trying to change the subject whenever Judith brought it up.

They'd walked over to a K Street restaurant called Jean Valjean, where Charlie had ordered a rare strip steak and Judith a shrimp salad. During a friendly lull between courses, while Judith was describing a car she intended to buy, a Camry, and Charlie interrupted her to bring up the fate of Robert Bork, who had decided to fight on for confirmation to the Supreme Court, Judith noticed that Charlie was studying an underdressed woman at a nearby table. The woman reminded Charlie of Virginia Mayo, whom he had recently seen in a film on channel five with, he believed, Farley Granger and Broderick Crawford. They had been held hostage by mobsters in a Cleveland luncheonette.

"Every man in this place is staring," Judith said when she saw where Charlie was looking.

"With damn good reason," he replied, attempting his most winning smile, much like the one that Crawford had attempted with Mayo. "I know it's pathetic."

But as Charlie uttered these words, he saw how Judith's lips appeared to stiffen and how a sort of transparent mask altered her face. As he tried to repair the last sentence, he understood that he ought to shut up, that she was not going to be sympathetic to his somewhat rambling explication: that such sights were merely an innocent pleasure. Of course he had every right to say what he felt, and he kept talking until he noticed that Judith's expression was still changing; there was something in it now—a darkening—he could not understand. Then the atmosphere became, if anything, worse: when Charlie hurriedly returned to the subject of the lawsuit and expressed his view that the doctrine of laches applied to mineral claims on the property in question, adding only that the issues were hopelessly tiresome, he made the very bad guess that, on that topic at least, she would commiserate.

A waiter came by to fill their water glasses, and by the time he'd left with his icy pitcher, Judith Grust's brown eyes looked opaque and small. "I don't know why you're telling me this," she said. "If you're burned out and bored by our work, that's a problem between you and the partners. I don't know why you thought I'd be interested in what turns a middle-aged man on. The truth is I find that kind of staring at women deeply offensive." She paused and added softly, "I'm sorry if I sound as if I'm lecturing you."

Charlie looked at his luncheon companion, and although his appetite had fled, he nibbled on a warm roll he'd already broken into two, then three and four pieces. Was she kidding? He searched her expression, hoping to find a trace of self-mockery. He found nothing of the sort. He tried to remember something witty that Broderick Crawford had said to Virginia Mayo: that if he were a dog and she were a steak, he wouldn't care, or something to that effect; and Virginia Mayo had said that he *was* a dog, mangy and dumb and flea-bitten, and then Crawford and Mayo had laughed together in the way that friends in mortal danger laugh.

"All I can say in my defense," Charlie said, as if he were seeking her vote, "is that I meant no harm in what I said. I was just being a guy. I mean, what are we coming to if we can't be honest about that?"

His apology, like heavy food, sank in his stomach.

"I just like women," he went on, producing what he believed was his most charming expression, far better than Broderick Crawford's best.

"It's been my experience," Judith Grust replied, her voice a little gentler, "that many men who talk about liking women are those most prone to committing violence against women. I hope you don't take this personally; I'm not suggesting that you're a violent person. But it's what I believe."

Their food arrived, and Judith seemed to stare with disapproval at Charlie's steaming plate of steak with béarnaise sauce and potatoes. Charlie forced out a new smile, as if to add a dash of gaiety to their table. "Got to lose some weight," he said, patting his stomach, and in the silence that followed, he glanced once more at the woman nearby who had set the whole thing off. A thin film of perspiration was visible, a dewy coating on pale cleavage. Charlie widened his eyes and, in a jumpy gesture, looked at his watch.

"My gosh!" he said. "I have an appointment back at the office in ten minutes. How could I possibly have allowed such a scheduling botch? Forgive me!" Overcome with regret, he waved for the check, brandishing his amber American Express card. Moments later he stood and bowed slightly, in almost military fashion.

That should have been enough, Charlie thought later, but he felt rattled by Judith Grust's contemptuous look, and as he completed his bow, he felt a powerful urge to try to heal the mysterious wound that he'd inflicted. As he bent his head to apologize again, he sniffed strong perfume and noticed pale fuzz on her cheeks. He felt foolish just standing there and deployed his absolutely vintage grin.

"You know," he whispered, "I worry that if I were a mangy dog and you were roast beef, I wouldn't care," realizing even as the words came out that perhaps he had gotten something terribly wrong, that the joke had been mangled irreparably. Virginia Mayo would not have enjoyed this repartee—not at all—and Broderick Crawford would never have said such a thing. What on earth was he thinking? "I was trying to make a stupid joke, and it came out all wrong," Charlie said hurriedly, but Judith Grust's brown eyes had become black ice, as if she were another hostile Pennsylvania voter ready to do him in.

TWO

Aᴏᴛᴇʀ Cʜᴀʀʟɪᴇ Dɪɴɢʟᴇᴍᴀɴ'ѕ ᴅᴇғᴇᴀᴛ in 1984, he returned
to the practice of law, becoming "of counsel" for Thingeld, Pine &
Sconce. Much of his job required a simple talent—making telephone calls to influential people who knew his name—and Charlie
was a little embarrassed by this line of work. He also was weary of
telling people that it was "great being back in the private sector" and
"wonderful to have time to see friends and family." He realized that
each time another group of former officeholders entered the job
market, he became slightly less employable.

By the fall of 1987 Charlie was forty-eight years old and earning
$215,000 a year. On his desk he kept the gavel he'd gotten as rank-
ing minority member of the Fisheries Management subcommittee,
and he sometimes tapped his desk with it, wondering what had
become of the nation's fish stocks without his attention. He was
miserable at Thingeld, Pine, and so apparently were the nearly two
hundred other lawyers around him. One partner, a gray-haired wid-
ower in his early sixties named Alfred Schmalz, looked about to
weep whenever someone spoke to him. Sometimes, when Schmalz
left his door open, Charlie could see him at his desk, hunched over,
rubbing his lower lip, which had a purplish discoloration. Another
partner had an oral twitch; after every sentence he'd say, "Oh yeah,
yup, yup!" and it was hard to avoid the one who kept muttering
"Fuckingassholes, fuckingassholes" as he walked around with his

head bent. In the last three years two partners and one associate had been taken away by ambulance (two false alarms and one real heart attack) and another partner, a man in his late forties, had died in the elevator on his way to court. With good cheer this doomed man had waved good-bye to the receptionist, and when the elevator door reopened at the lobby, passengers on their way up discovered the body on the floor. They were in a hurry and didn't mind having the dead man along for the ride.

Thingeld, Pine was near the corner of Seventeenth and K streets, in a ten-story building with a design so assertively mediocre that passersby sometimes felt an inexplicable urge to cross the street. The top two floors belonged to Thingeld, Pine, and the rest of the building was leased to a data processing firm, two "investigative" journalists, four associations representing the interests of toxic or otherwise harmful products, and a travel agency that was believed to be a front for Burmese intelligence. Charlie would shake his head when he thought how his days had become entwined with this place, where bank fraud and tax law and incomprehensible legislation and wills and trusts occupied their time. Charlie believed that boredom was the secret curse of his generation. This was not so simple as what magazine writers liked to call a "midlife episode." Rather it was a sense of inescapable repetition as all of them edged toward their inevitable end. This grim outlook made Charlie unusually receptive when he got the news that he was going to be offered a job in the White House.

Charlie heard this from his best friend in Washington, a six-term California congressman and former neighbor named Fred Hykler, who called him from the House gymnasium. Fred was not precisely sure what the job was, but he knew it came with a good title—assistant to the president—and Charlie felt enormous relief at this prospect. He was sure that it would help him to sort out all the misplaced pieces of his recent life. "Just sit tight," Fred told him, and went on to say that the White House wanted someone just like Charlie, someone who had been around and was not uncomfortable with the philosophy of Ronald Reagan. In Washington people used the word "philosophy" to refer to any thoughts that seemed to connect to one another, however briefly.

This conversation cheered up Charlie so much that he called the firm's last living founding partner, Anthony "Pete" Thingeld.

"I have a moment right now," Thingeld said, almost eagerly, Charlie thought, and he met Charlie outside his office, clutched Charlie's elbow, and led him inside. As Thingeld closed the door firmly behind, he said, "I can imagine what this is about."

Charlie could not imagine how Thingeld had already heard about his prospects, although the old partner—a former deputy attorney general—was still in touch with much of Washington. Perhaps, though, he hadn't heard, Charlie thought, because Thingeld looked surprised, then oddly pleased, when Charlie said that he might be leaving, and he seemed enthusiastic even though Charlie could not be specific about what he'd actually be doing so late in Reagan's second term. As Charlie heard his own voice, he knew that he did not sound as confident as he'd wanted to, and he sensed that Thingeld, who had not invited him to sit, wanted a quick conversation.

"This is very good news for us," the founding partner told Charlie, scratching his head, flakes of dandruff coming off his pink scalp. When Charlie did not know how to interpret this, Thingeld said, "What I mean to say is that it's grand to have our people in the thick of things."

"I could be there," Charlie said.

"It's been a long time for me," Thingeld said, pointing at his wall of pictures of himself. "I'm through in this town. When I was your age, I swore I'd never become someone like me."

"Don't underrate yourself," Charlie said. "Everybody in this town still knows your name."

"Not anymore." The founding partner seemed to chew his own tongue before saying, "I wonder why we keep calling this frightful place 'this town,' anyway. Who started that?"

"Beats me," Charlie said.

"You'll have to cut your ties with us," Thingeld said—a little too quickly, Charlie thought.

"I'm not leaving yet," Charlie said. "There's nothing official."

"Of course, of course, you just wanted me to know, and I heard you."

Charlie was sorry that he'd told Thingeld anything.

"It might make that little problem with that woman go away," Thingeld said, and Charlie was not quite sure that he'd heard correctly.

"What problem?" he asked, and felt his heart speed up ever so slightly.

"She seems to have it in for you," Thingeld said. "She's something of a fanatic; she's talked to me twice. I thought that's why you wanted to talk."

"Judith Grust," Charlie said.

"Something like that," the founding partner said. "Snippy bitch, whatever. A damned hard worker though."

Thingeld went on to call Judith a "pain in the ass," while adding that she was "smart as a whip—that's why we want to keep her. She'll make partner for sure." And (it was as if the subject hadn't changed) he went on to say, a little mysteriously, "It might not be a bad idea to telephone some psychiatrist, just to show you're aware of things, Charlie, if you get my drift."

"You're not serious, Pete," Charlie said.

"Oh, I wouldn't worry," the founding partner replied. He had already revealed that Charlie had been under unusual pressure and that (this fib was vouchsafed to Judith in absolute confidence) Charlie was meeting regularly with a specialist to deal with a personal problem that was of no small concern to the partners. He patted Charlie softly on the back, explaining that after a lifetime in the business, he knew when a lie worked better than the truth, and he knew the wisdom of telling precisely the lie that the recipient wanted to hear. Then they shook hands, their clasp lingering a second or two beyond what was usual.

. . .

AT THE END of the day Charlie ran for a descending elevator, and it was only when the door squeezed shut that he realized he was once more alone with Judith Grust. She looked away and Charlie, because he couldn't help himself, looked at her legs and then forced his eyes upward. Judith was wearing a blue blazer and blue skirt and, now, a shocked expression. When Charlie considered that this very person had denounced him, he bit his lip; when he heard his voice, words came out that seemed to have almost no connection to his thoughts. It was as if a third party were speaking.

"I'm truly sorry, Miss Grust, if I did anything to offend you," the speaker said as the door flung itself wide to expose the lobby. Charlie produced yet another top-notch smile from his repertoire. "I'm really ashamed at the way I sounded, which I hope you know I didn't mean."

"The important thing is that you're getting help," she said, her jaw clenched. "People should always get help with their problems." Then, for the moment, they went their separate ways.

THREE

Henry (Hank) Morriday gave a lot of thought to what he'd do when the Democrats ran the country again. He saw his office at the Institute, where he was a Fellow, as a sort of waiting room, but as the years passed and new Fellows showed up, he had become increasingly impatient to move on.

Hank had just turned forty, and this new decade made him more restless. There were days when he couldn't absorb another cup of the coffee from the office urn, which left him vaguely ill. He found it harder to go to the lunches sponsored by the Institute, where unfailingly a panel would talk about urban crime or monetary policy or the challenge of China's labor force. He got no more pleasure from his dark green BMW 325is than he'd gotten from the light blue Chevy Nova he'd parted with—even a bit less, for he'd never worried about the Nova getting scratched when he'd left it on the street or when a parking attendant zipped off. Women seemed no more impressed by the BMW 325is than by anything else about him, and a book he was writing wasn't going well at all.

The Institute, close to Dupont Circle, was populated by people that the world had lost track of, such as a former deputy secretary of state, two doors down from Hank, and a former budget analyst across the hall. Many Fellows were, like Hank, known only to those who studied the same policy questions, often at places like the Institute. Hank had once worked for the congressman who represented the Upper West Side of Manhattan, and he'd become the staff expert on welfare reform, which was the subject of his book; he got to visit Camp David for a welfare seminar and, after a fashion, carved a small, impermanent notch in urban policy thought. But his congressman had suddenly retired, and Hank knew that he'd been lucky to end up at the Institute.

At first he did what he could to remind people that he existed; he appeared on local news programs and PBS and wrote an attack on the welfare system that, inexplicably, appeared twice in *The Washington Post*. By the fall of 1987 though, demand for Hank had fallen off, and he envied other Fellows, such as a Soviet specialist named Suzanne Smule, who was said to be close to important Democrats and was on television all the time. In the early afternoon a visitor to the Institute might hear only the *click, click* of keyboards as Fellows took stock of the nation and the world. Listening to that *click, click*, there were times when Hank Morriday could barely concentrate on his book, with its single mothers and broken families and its "cycles," and he would put his head in his hands and more or less count the days until Reagan's second term was done.

Hank's social life had verged on the disastrous. The worst thing had been his evening out with Jennifer, a researcher at the Institute. Hank had sensed in Jennifer a sweet vapidity, and before asking her out, he had thought a lot about her pink skin, the chubby smoothness at her elbows, and the moment when she would gaze at him, her eyes slightly crossed, and ask about a knotty policy question. If his pursuit seemed to be going well (and for a week or so he had stopped by her desk to chat), he would tell her about his visit to Camp David. Hank had no idea that Jennifer saw him as someone who couldn't stop talking about himself. She had said yes, finally, to dinner, because she'd had nothing else to do that night, and afterward she wasn't paying much attention when Hank came into her apartment in Friendship Heights, promising to make a phone call and leave. But once there Hank had made a terrible mistake. He had tried to kiss Jennifer, and as his lips brushed hers, he believed that her little giggle was a sound of pleasure, which persuaded him to try again. "Give me a break," she'd said.

"There's a big dinner next week at the Institute," Hank said. "The president of Mozambique, or Belgium, one of those, and I was going to ask you."

Jennifer looked at him with neither sweetness nor vapidity. "I have to work," she said. "I have to work every day for the rest of your life."

Hank smiled then, because her words sounded so extreme. But in less than three minutes Hank was on the street, trying to remember where he'd left his car.

He managed to blot this erratic behavior from memory, and within a week or so he almost believed that he could persuade Jennifer to go out again, perhaps to a new Mongolian restaurant in Georgetown. But he also knew better and was a little relieved when she quit her job and went to business school in Boston. For two months after that Hank's only dates had been with a lawyer named Judith Grust. They'd met at a reception for one of Hank's Swarthmore classmates, someone who'd just published a book about government paperwork that Washington reviewers had called "trenchant." Two dozen people had shown up in the living room of a row house in Burleith, where a green sofa had been shredded by a nasty-looking brown cat that finally leaped onto the pile of neglected books. At first Hank was not drawn to the thin woman with dark, alert eyes, but she wasn't bad. Judith had a similar response to the man with the beard who kept looking elsewhere, although when he came over to talk, gnawing on celery and carrot sticks, she thought that he was working too hard to impress her.

Since then they had been together three times, and their outings so far had not been a lot of fun. When they talked about welfare or criminal justice, they would challenge each other's statistics. Once, when he'd taken her hand as they crossed a street, her hand seemed to change into something else. It felt oddly heavier, as if it had fallen asleep.

The last time they'd gone out, after a long dinner Hank had wheeled them about town, and moments after they'd pulled up in front of the arched entrance to her apartment building on California Street, he had looped his arm around her shoulder, hoping for a sign of affection. "Don't," she said, and only when Hank retreated sulkily behind the steering wheel did her tone become warmer. She told him that she wasn't angry, but she did want him to know that she could become so.

Why did he persist in asking her out? Hank supposed it was because Judith seemed to take him seriously; because they understood one another, perhaps too well; and because he was fairly certain that he could get Judith to sleep with him, although even that possibility did not excite him much: she was too thin and too shrewd, not at all like Jennifer the researcher. Yet Hank was aware that abstinence makes the world lovelier, and that fall, when he thought about how to spend an evening, Judith Grust's was the only name that came to mind.

FOUR

On a late night in early November, Charlie Dingleman paced around his living room and waited for Eve, his wife, to get home. Eve had started law school in September, and although Charlie had liked the idea, now she was never home. As he paced, he watched the eleven o'clock news; Reynolds Mund, his favorite local anchorman, looked fidgety, which is why Charlie liked watching him. Tonight Mund was reporting details of a double homicide in the Southeast section of the city, and as he did so, Charlie's anxious imagination came up with images of a murdered spouse. Then Mund talked about a tractor trailer that had created "havoc" on the Beltway, tipping over and spreading its "possibly deadly cargo." There seemed to be a gleam of pleasure in his eyes as he went on about this, and Charlie realized that he was feeling a certain satisfaction too.

Charlie's anxious mood wasn't helped by the fact that a man named Skip Haine, who worked for the White House personnel office, hadn't returned his call from the early afternoon. Just the other day, Charlie had woken up at four A.M., sure that the White House job had never been for real, that his name had been mentioned as a mere gesture; and as the green-blue numbers on his clock radio formed new patterns, like insects breeding, he understood that Washington was perhaps above all a universe of gestures.

He was sleeping badly anyway, and it didn't help that Eve sighed demonstratively and turned over whenever he reached out to her. Sometimes he went downstairs to watch overnight movies; channel five had been showing films of Second World War vintage, and a particular favorite starred James Cagney trying to get out of Tokyo, pursued by lisping Japanese agents. Charlie knew just how Cagney felt—ill-wishers lurking on every corner, people not unlike those Pennsylvanians who never cared how much he'd cared, *really* cared, about their jobs, their homes, their values (a bumper sticker had said, "He Values Your Values"); and people like Judith Grust. Weeks after his lunch with Judith, Charlie still could not grasp that she'd actually complained about him to the last founding partner.

Charlie had never liked their living room, which Eve had turned into a replica of one that she'd seen in *Architectural Digest*, including the Cabestan rug and the rosewood bookcase that held biographies of warranted statesmen (Churchill, Roosevelt), the collected words of Daniel Boorstin, the memoirs of White House lieutenants (George Reedy, Theodore Sorensen), a few volumes of popular fiction (James Clavell, Erica Jong). The ficus tree, close to death, was also her doing.

When Charlie heard a taxi door slam, it was past one-thirty—after the news he had gone to Johnny Carson and thence to David Letterman—and he'd begun more seriously to consider the possibility that something bad had happened. Washington was not a safe place; people in the law office made terse references to "the blacks" and looked over their shoulders to be sure they were not overheard by one of the four blacks who worked there (one of whom was Charlie's secretary, Tonya). He peered through a slit in the venetian blind and saw that indeed it was his wife.

When Eve came through the door, Charlie found himself unable at first to speak. When he said something, it was "Where the hell have you been?" She looked at him coldly and her first, uncoded words were "Charlie, I guess we have to talk," followed by "You're trying to sit on me, and I don't know if I can stand it much longer."

They stared at each other. The lipstick on her large mouth looked bright.

"You're my wife," Charlie said, wishing that the television weren't so loud and that he'd managed to come up with something more original.

"Don't call me 'your wife,'" she replied. "I'm not your anything."

With that she walked across the Cabestan and clumped up the stairs, making, Charlie thought, much more noise than a woman so tiny ought to make. A moment later he followed her into the bedroom, which was filled by a king-sized bed, two end tables that the salesman had called Spanish modern, and another television, this one with a nineteen-inch screen.

"Tell me what it is you're trying to say," he said.

"What I'm saying, Charlie," she said, falling to the bed as if it were a trampoline, "is that it's very, very late, and you have to be at work tomorrow, and I have a very, very difficult exam coming up, and I want to go to sleep."

"I'll bet you do," he said.

"You're behaving stupidly," she said.

"I'm behaving," Charlie said, a little too plaintively, he knew, "like someone trying to figure out the woman he fell in love with"— though he felt no affection for her at this moment and hadn't for a while—"and married." And left his family for, although he didn't say that; he would never have left, he was sure, if Abigail, his first wife, had forgiven him, which he didn't say either.

"There's nothing to figure out," Eve said without inflection, her tongue licking her lower lip. "We're both tired. If you're not going to bed, I am."

Rather than going to bed, Charlie, who was agitated, returned to the living room and tried to remember what they'd just said. Perhaps he had overstepped some line? He heard the upstairs bathroom door close and a burst of water and then a faint trickle. He knew her habits: by now she'd be wearing panties and her favorite T-shirt, one she'd kept from Bruce Springsteen's "The River" tour, another reminder of the twenty years between them. At moments like this Charlie wanted to telephone his ex-wife and talk about his problems. But then he would remember how miserable Abigail had been after they'd moved to Washington. She had put on thirty pounds and begun to wear the same pale green nightgown every night and left a permanent pile of clothing by her side of the bed. Abigail always wanted to watch Johnny Carson to the very end, when the people on Johnny's couch chatted soundlessly. She was always letting him know that he'd missed some irretrievable event involving the children. That was her talent, he used to say when they fought: making him feel rotten.

By contrast Eve DeFole, whom Charlie hired as a legislative assistant in his third term, seemed only to admire him. She was barely five feet tall, her mouth was large, out of proportion to the rest of her, and a pointed nose gave her, in the eyes of strangers, a sharp aspect. She made Charlie feel perpetually clumsy, especially when she forced him to breathe her perfume and smiled widely up at him. When he'd hired Eve, part of him had wished that she wouldn't wear those short, flaring skirts, which showed off her perfect, almost delicate legs, but Charlie never said anything. One night in his outsized office, when the sounds of a cleaning crew seemed far away, Eve and Charlie had been talking about essential fish habitats in large inland waterways. When she handed Charlie a pencil, she absentmindedly (so he imagined) left her hand at the top of his left leg. Moments later she removed her hand, and then Charlie put it back.

He had not wanted the divorce, but how could he have told that to his constituents? How could he have explained that yes, sure, true enough, he had moved out, but that his wife, the former Abigail Smith, had been the merciless one? How could he explain that it was Abigail who had shrieked at him and used words like "betrayal," not he, and that it was she who had ordered him to go. Yet even while Charlie was actually moving out of their four-bedroom house in McLean, he could not quite believe that he was doing so; and even after Eve moved in with him, in the narrow town house that he'd bought on R Street, in Georgetown, there were times when he imagined that he could just go home to Abigail, although he more or less dropped that idea at about the time that he married Eve.

Charlie sometimes wondered what Abigail would think if he were killed, say in a plane crash. What would she regret not having told him—what final, tender words? He would wonder (sometimes his eyes would become quite moist) what his own last thoughts of Abigail might be. On this particular late night in November, as Charlie stared at the moribund ficus in the living room, he found himself wishing that the person climbing into bed upstairs was not the tiny woman with a sharp nose and a pretty body who no longer smiled at him but her predecessor.

FIVE

Oₙₑ ᴅᴀʏ ᴀᴛ the Institute Hank Morriday spotted someone who looked like Robert S. McNamara but an older version; then he realized that it *was* McNamara who was shuffling off to the men's room. This McNamara was not only grayer than the slick, black-haired miscreant he'd used to be, but there was a liquid quality to his features; around his eyes, when Hank stared for a moment, Robert McNamara seemed to be dissolving.

Hank knew that he ought to be making more progress on his book, but his mind wandered. It had taken nearly three years to fin-ish the first two hundred pages, a comparison of the way Europe and the United States treated their poor and "unemployable." In his mind Hank had worked out a plea for reform, but he worried that his plea was not wholly fresh; when people asked, he would usually say that he hoped to "arrive at a few useful insights." Also he would sometimes think about all those people who couldn't hold real jobs and realize that he could not imagine holding one of those jobs him-self. In any case Hank found it increasingly hard to concentrate on his project, and too often he locked his office and read newspapers and spy novels and thought about a future in the next administra-tion. In the evening, when he was alone and knew that he ought to be working, he often watched television, especially his favorite, *Per-fect Fit*, which was set in a fashion designer's studio. Hank adored the star of the program, an actress named Wendy Lullabay; in the opening credits she wore several outfits, including white tennis shorts, a tiny black dress, and, as she frolicked on a California beach, an azure bikini. More often than not Wendy was far more interesting to Hank Morriday than any book he might conceivably write.

Every so often the director of the Institute, Randolph Maintree, would materialize in a doorway. There was something about Randolph Maintree that made Hank uneasy. Part of it perhaps was the director's reputation as a sage, for he was someone who had repeatedly served as a special envoy during the first decades of the Cold War. Part of it was his deep, smooth voice and his appearance: Randolph Maintree was a large man with hair that is often described as silver but is, rather, a paling yellow, which in his case curled thickly around a face that is often described as rugged but was, in his case, simply covered with deep creases.

"How goes it, Henry?" the director would ask with a smile that Hank could never interpret.

"Fine, I believe, just fine" was Hank's standard reply, accompanied usually by a weak grin and a stroking of his beard.

"And how goes the work?"

"Always a struggle," Hank would reply.

"Do us proud, Henry," the director would say, offering his muscular hand for a shake. Maintree would then stroll off to perform much the same dialogue at another office, with men and women who'd once held jobs that were far more important than Hank's.

Then one afternoon Hank found himself studying an issue of *Playboy*, which he'd bought because it promised pictures of Wendy Lullabay. On one page Wendy had taken off her bikini and wore only wet, clinging sand. Back and forth Hank went—with bikini and without—and after a few minutes, when he started to hold the magazine upside down as if to shake away the sand clumps, Randolph Maintree knocked sharply on his door and almost simultaneously walked in. Hank dropped the magazine to the floor, kicking it under his desk, and the director seemed not to notice. But for the first time Maintree did not offer his firm hand for a shake, did not ask how the work was going, and he left Hank feeling no longer as welcome as he had been.

.   .   .

JUST THE OTHER DAY Hank had telephoned the one woman in Washington who could be relied upon to go out with him on short notice. But when he'd called, she had sounded less enthusiastic than she had the last time.

"Hank, I'm very busy; what is it?" Judith Grust said after he'd been put on hold and had waited nearly five minutes for her to return to the phone.

Hank looked at his watch; it was six-thirty, and much of the city had started home, loosing great blue clouds of exhaust to settle in a bubble around them all.

"I'll be wrapping up here pretty soon, and I thought about, you know, dinner," he said with a half-yawn.

"I'm going to be here late, Hank," she said, and he could hear impatience in her voice. "I'm way behind."

"What," he asked, "do you mean by late?"

"I mean I don't know." She paused, as if calculating the effect of her words. "Of course I'd love to see you," she added, as if in apology. "I might be done by eight. Could you wait?"

She saw through him! Sometimes it was as if everybody on the planet saw through him.

"Sure, that would work out fine with my schedule here," he said with some heartiness.

Hank, who knew that he'd not been clever, left the office to stroll along Connecticut Avenue, browsing in a record store (buying, finally, a CD to replace a Band album he hadn't listened to in years, suspecting that the CD would go unplayed too) and after that a bookstore (almost getting a volume in his field, then deciding he would not give a rival one more sale). Then in a decisive instant—just as he was about to study the window display of a darkened clothing store—Hank spotted a pay phone and called Judith.

"You know, something has come up," he told her with regret and secret triumph.

"Actually, there's something I want to talk to you about that is important," she said mysteriously, and proposed lunch on the following day.

"Give me a hint," Hank said.

"I don't want to on the phone," she replied even more mysteriously. "But it's about someone who works here. It's someone who I'm starting to think shouldn't work here—or anywhere that's important."

SIX

THE NEXT DAY, when Hank Morriday spun through the revolving door of the Thingeld, Pine & Sconce building, with lunchtime office workers spinning out, Judith Grust was already waiting in the lobby. She seemed jumpy and wiggled her fingers as she looked around. In the door Hank watched his reflection and wondered if his beard made him look older or younger than his forty years.

They headed for Barkley's, a restaurant named after Truman's vice president, a large room off Connecticut Avenue where tourists peeked inside just to see the totems listed in guidebooks: one of Walter Johnson's uniforms, a stuffed dog that had belonged to William Howard Taft, photographs signed by John Kennedy and Sam Rayburn, a life-sized wax figure of John Foster Dulles. When one entered Barkley's, a great chattering noise rose up in greeting, and when Hank and Judith arrived, clusters of customers were pushing each other, standing on tiptoe as if to search for cleared tables. Hank spotted a senior Fellow from the Institute and waved to him with a wink. He smiled comfortably, at peace, briefly, with this world.

Judith, he thought, looked attractive, and she took his arm as they walked to their table. Moments later, just as she reached for an oblong roll covered with sesame seeds, the diners around them stirred slightly. In this case they had noticed Reynolds Mund, the popular local anchorman, who was being guided by the maitre d' to a table in the center of the room.

"I should maybe say hello," Hank said to Judith, sounding as offhand as he possibly could. Mund's television station, he explained, sometimes called him for an expert opinion, although it had been a while. "When they get stuck on welfare issues," he added with weary modesty, stroking his beard.

Judith looked reflective and bit into a breadstick; powdery crumbs sprayed around her mouth and a few clung to her lower lip. Hank looked into her dark, intelligent eyes. He wished that he had amusing stories to tell her, anecdotes that he'd not used up on their first date. Phrases like "setting a course of no return" and "Harris has signed off on that" made their way about the restaurant, blending with the crunch of breadsticks and the slurps of soft food.

"So, how are things with you?" he asked.

"You don't want to know."

Hank was instantly attentive, and he tried to follow what Judith was telling him about a tragic crash in the law firm's computer system (who knew what was lost!), although his mind wandered. He felt his knee touching Judith's lower thigh, and the thought of this, a mystery of nearby anatomy, warmed him. He moved his leg very slightly, which he knew could be interpreted as a rubbing motion, but risked it anyway. When Judith asked him how his work was going, Hank watched her stare at a faraway place.

"Most of the time," he said confidingly, sensing that she wasn't paying attention, "it's an isolated kind of life. You sit there trying to organize your thoughts, wondering if you really will make a difference." She nodded, as he had nodded, at regular intervals. "Also," he said, shaking his head as he changed the subject, "I want to be involved, but I don't know. Maybe Mario Cuomo will run." She nodded again, and when he sensed that she had stopped listening entirely, he said, "But you wanted to talk about something."

A waiter who was bent at a forty-five-degree angle brought them a fresh basket of rolls, steam rising through a white napkin. For a while Judith said nothing; her mouth was full. But then she began to tell Hank about someone at her firm. When she mentioned Charlie Dingleman's name, Hank had a vague memory of a red-faced Pennsylvanian who'd served on a committee (something to do with protecting fish) with Hank's congressman and had always seemed pleasant enough.

She lowered her voice to a whisper; her knee seemed to press in response to his. "He's a pathological case," she told him.

"Meaning . . .?"

"Meaning he's been told to get help for his sexual disorder, or else."

These words were so whispery and rushed that Hank was not sure that he'd heard correctly.

"My first lunch with him," she continued in a whisper, "he was using the power thing—you know, former congressman, hungry associate. I was extremely angry at him for that. Then he said something—something horrible. I can't repeat it. But I left with the feeling that he was someone capable of violence against women." She paused. "Something about raw meat," she added, closing her eyes at the memory.

Hank nodded sympathetically, each nod signaling his total agreement, although he still had no idea what this was about.

"I think he was just there for a couple of terms and then he lost," Hank said. "Maybe three." He wondered if Judith was aware that their bare skins were separated only by layers of cloth.

"He reminded me of this law professor I had who called me into his office and, out of the blue, grabbed me," Judith said. Hank moved his knee away, as gently as possible. Moments later, though, their knees touched once more, and this time the motion came from her side of the table, definitely. Hank noticed that their waiter, who seemed to be in pain, was tapping his pencil, waiting for their order. They asked for crab cakes, a specialty at Barkley's.

Hank was also trying to overhear a conversation at a nearby table that mentioned "the senator" and which he imagined had something to do with the 1988 presidential race. He had no idea what this Dingleman person had actually done, and he wanted to learn more about Judith's professor. As she spoke, she seemed less tense; her brown eyes looked gentler; there was a flush on her cheeks as she told him about the teacher. "He suddenly put his hand on my genitalia," she said. "It gave me the most horrible, helpless, violated feeling, because he was somebody I really had admired. I felt so degraded. And I was very young; I was afraid to do anything, so I did nothing."

Hank felt oddly excited when she introduced her genitalia into the conversation. He was also trying to figure out who "the senator" was; two ears weren't enough. Now Judith was telling him that a year later that same professor had called to apologize; Hank noticed for the first time that the veins in Judith's arms were very near the surface. "But then he helped me get an internship in Philadelphia and I saw how sorry he was," she said softly. "And I forgave him."

A few minutes later Judith leaned closer to Hank to say more, lowering her voice as their waiter plunked down more rolls. In a shrill whisper she told Hank that this Charlie Dingleman had been offered an important job at the White House. "That really bothers me," she said.

"You should be happy that he's leaving the firm, if he annoys you so much," Hank said, noticing that the nearby senior Fellow seemed to be staring at them with grim intensity. What was that guy working on? Hank could not remember, but someone had told him that he was very close to Dick Gephardt, or someone who might go far.

"Don't be stupid," Judith said. Hank looked around nervously as she scolded him and went on, "I'm not talking about my feelings. I'm talking about the fact that a man who has acknowledged that he's suffering from a major sexual disorder is going to work in a sensitive job for the president of the United States!"

"What do you mean by a major sexual disorder?" Hank whispered, pleased at the increasing intimacy of their conversation.

"I believe he's hoping to take this problem with him to the White House," Judith replied.

"That's a very serious thing," Hank said, whispering directly into Judith's ear, which he thought was beautifully shaped. "But I mean you don't actually seem to know what the trouble is, if you don't mind my saying so. Maybe it's some personal thing? What do you think?" he persisted, as two plates of crab cakes with astounding speed were brought and flung before them as if they were stubborn children.

"It's not a limp dick," Judith said, her voice a little louder, and Hank blushed, reminded that his own dick had not had a chance to audition for Judith. "I wish you were a little smarter about the implications of things like this," she added.

Judith speared a piece of crab cake, losing a gob of tartar sauce down the front of her blouse. "Damn!" she said, dipping a napkin into her glass of ice water, enlarging the spot. Then she pursed her lips and stared brightly at Hank as she whispered, "He's getting a job in maybe the most important place in the world and you honestly don't know what I'm *talking* about?"

Judith's face reddened, and she fastened a napkin around her neck, protecting her blouse from further droppings. Then she looked past Hank toward Reynolds Mund, whose luncheon companions were a New England senator and a bitter-faced newspaper columnist named Brandon Sladder, who often appeared on television and had mastered the ominous phrase "This may turn out to be really interesting." Judith was whispering again, her voice an agi-

tated, angry sibilance, and Hank thought how it was possible to dis-
like a person and nevertheless put a hand on that person's knee and
rub it. She asked Hank if he could help her do something about
Charlie Dingleman—not for her, but for the country. She pointed
toward Reynolds Mund. "You know that world, Hank," she said ad-
miringly. She pressed her hand on top of his and squeezed. Hank
quite naturally squeezed back, and then he smiled and waved at
Reynolds Mund, who did not seem to have any idea who Hank was.

SEVEN

Teresa Maracopulos sometimes thought that she was missing out on everything that made it interesting to be part of her place and time, and this depressed her. Teresa was thirty-two. She was short and a little chubby and sometimes had a puzzled expression, as if she was always missing the point of a joke. She sometimes could not remember why she'd married Martin Himmelschaft, her husband of six years, who worked downtown in the District government's personnel office. Martin was forty-four; his skin was chalky and he looked perpetually fatigued. He had not wanted Teresa to keep her unmarried name, but she had won that argument because it was the name that she had at her office.

While most of their friends lived west of Rock Creek Park, Teresa and Martin lived in a two-bedroom town house on the fringes of Capitol Hill, actually Fifteenth Street, Northeast, a block occasionally visited by the gunfire, which in that decade had become part of Washington life. Teresa was afraid of the neighborhood, but Martin was weary of explaining why it made no sense to move: the real estate market had stalled and they would not make a cent on their investment of $14,000 down on a $70,000 house that ought to sell for $110,000, as Martin had it figured, but would get them less than $70,000 the way things were now.

Teresa did not argue because Martin took care of their money, and Teresa had long ago deduced that her husband was a cheapskate.

They had not in any case had many serious conversations, although now and then they talked about having a child. Many of the people they saw at their offices had children, and sometimes when they watched television, they would imagine how nice it would be to watch television with their child.

Martin, as an administrator in the personnel office, earned $42,600 dollars a year and had no hope of earning much more unless he left the government, which would mean losing many accumulated benefits. Teresa earned $28,000 as an assistant account executive at Big Tooth, the public relations firm where she'd been for nine years; it was the only real job she'd ever had. Despite her title she knew that she was little more than a secretary. She had been told by a partner not to expect a lot more, so Teresa's choice was to leave or to stay in a job that would come to seem increasingly humble.

But Teresa could not bear to give up her ties to an office whose name and symbol—two front teeth sunk into the planet Earth—were so widely known. Big Tooth clients included whole countries as well as corrupt officials, second-tier movie stars, and one former president; its very name not only guaranteed reservations at any restaurant but carried with it the promise of resurrection or, in some cases, obscurity. Teresa would miss that feeling of importance in a life that, as time passed, left her feeling increasingly unimportant.

Teresa suspected that she got more sustenance from Big Tooth than from married life. At the end of a day it was more fun to have a drink with friends from the office than to go home and walk the scary streets. She felt close to her office friends, although she knew that if she were to leave Big Tooth, she would lose touch with them. She understood that they were work friends, even if they had much the same role to play as other friends. Like the friends she'd made in school, work friends sent you flowers if you went to the hospital or if someone died; they asked about your health and vacations and families; one could gossip with them and sometimes go to movies with them and even tell them real secrets.

Yet work friends, Teresa knew, vanished when they left the place where they'd worked together. She'd gone to office good-bye ceremonies, sometimes elaborate dinners and occasions of streaming tears and clutching hugs and generous gifts. When Teresa thought back on some of these farewells, she could still feel sad. But over the years she had noticed that these departing men and women never stayed in touch; they undoubtedly went on to make new work friends in their new places and then to forget the old ones. It was a lesson Teresa remembered whenever she thought about leaving Big Tooth: the people in her office were the best work friends she could ever imagine having and she never wanted to lose them.

. . .

WHEN TERESA came to work at nine, wearing the silver Big Tooth pin that all employees got after five years (an eighteen-karat gold model replaced it after ten years), she would get coffee at the office pot (skim milk, NutraSweet) and from there take a seat at the smaller of two desks in the office that she shared with her best work friend, an account executive named Candy Romulade.

It was a small office, and by late fall only flashes of sunlight made it through the windows. The senior account executives had larger offices, and the grandest of these belonged to Big Tooth's four founders: a former astronaut, a former senator, a former secretary of commerce, and a former presidential counselor, who hadn't been seen in years. Their rooms were located as if they were spokes on a great wheel, each with an outer door and an inner one that was connected to a spectacular conference room, a light-filled place where photographs of celebrated clients hung along the walls and two giant porcelain teeth hung from the ceiling.

On the day that Teresa Maracopulos met Reynolds Mund, the local anchorman, she was a little late to work, the parking garage at

Nineteenth and K streets having overfilled, and at 9:06 she rushed past the waiflike receptionist and went to her desk, flinging down her large purse. After telling Candy Romulade about the delay at the garage and watching Candy's face grow slack with boredom, Teresa made her way to the coffeepot, her shoes softly building up an electric charge on the gray carpet, and nodded to the anchorman. Reynolds Mund had stopped by Big Tooth's small studio to tape a public service announcement, a denunciation of drug use delivered in his most solemn voice. ("If you don't stop drugs, drugs will stop you." A soaring football was frozen in mid-spiral.) Teresa had seen lots of celebrities during her years at Big Tooth and was therefore surprised to find herself impressed. When he smiled at her just as he did on camera, she thought that she'd never seen such a warm, kind smile.

"Hey, I'd like some of that coffee too," he said in the raspy voice familiar to his viewers. When she handed him her own mug, with "Teresa" in delicate blue script along its creamy side, she thought that he looked handsomer than he did on the little screen.

"I promise to wash it," he said. "Ter-*e*-sa," he added, slowly reading aloud from the mug.

"You'd better," she replied flirtatiously, delighted by the warmth that she thought she saw in his eyes.

Teresa knew that Reynolds Mund was regularly honored by religious groups, interracial coalitions, and fraternal associations; he spoke at area schools and helped to sponsor a college scholarship in his name. People said that he had turned down network jobs because he believed it was his destiny to be part of Washington—a city, he often said, of real people. He was also a little mysterious. Not long before a reporter for a local magazine had gone to Mund's hometown in downstate Illinois and discovered that his real name was Malcolm Mund (a yearbook showed him with a crew cut) and that he was six years older (fifty-three) than he claimed to be. Malcolm's teachers remembered him as quiet and physically awkward but quick on his feet, and the journalist wrote about Mund's hometown in the language that is required of such articles: "It is a place where the man who owns the drugstore on Main Street is called Pop and the Rotary Club meets every Thursday at noon and the boy everyone knew as Mal Mund lived quietly with his parents in a modest, shingled house in a neighborhood of manicured green lawns and barking dogs." The writer, whose instinct for hidden stories was greater than her talent for writing them, believed there was much more to learn about her subject, but her editor had pushed her to finish and move on to something else: a fawning look at a headmaster whose school the editor wanted his son to attend.

As Teresa filled a Styrofoam cup with coffee for herself, she kept looking at this man with the great smile and crooked nose. She had heard of people having this effect on others, but it had never happened to her, and as he gulped coffee from her personal mug, Teresa thought that she would have to figure out a way to see him again.

A little later, when she saw the anchorman carrying a Burberry over his right arm, she told Candy that she wasn't feeling at all well and probably shouldn't have come in; she grabbed her coat and ran.

"Do I know you?" Reynolds Mund asked when she caught up with him as the elevator doors slid shut.

"Just in passing," Teresa replied.

As they walked together onto K Street (the yellow brick Big Tooth building was two blocks west of the Thingeld, Pine building; a preoccupied Charlie Dingleman passed in a hurry), Teresa told Reynolds how interesting it would be if someday she could watch him at work.

"It *is* interesting," the anchorman said, and seemed deep in thought.

"Can I give you a ride someplace?" she asked. "I'm getting my car."

"That would be a kindness," the anchorman said, almost as if he had expected the offer. "I came by taxi."

At the parking garage, where the attendant complained that Teresa had promised to leave her Subaru all day, she watched passersby stare at the anchorman and then inspect her. She tried to imagine how they looked as a couple and the more she thought about it, the harder it was not to feel a little smug.

EIGHT

Hank Morriday wished that Judith Grust wouldn't talk so much about that guy in her office, as if there were nothing else of importance in the world. "Maybe he'll reform," Hank said when they spoke on the phone a day or so after their lunch.

"Huh?" Judith replied after several seconds.

"I mean, people change," Hank assured her. He chuckled at the very thought of someone misbehaving near the Oval Office, but Judith didn't laugh with him.

"I have an idea," she said after another fairly long silence. "You should call Reynolds Mund. You told me you know him."

"Not all that well."

"Please make the call," Judith said.

Hank wished that he had never waved to the anchorman or told Judith about his rare television appearances.

"What exactly do you think I should tell him?" Hank asked.

"You've got to tell him about Charles Dingleman," she replied. "It's actually your duty as a citizen. You can be their secret source."

For several days Hank did nothing, but Judith had a way of provoking him. "You're afraid of something, aren't you?" she asked. By the time they'd made another date for dinner, she had turned this into a test that Hank didn't want to fail. So Hank finally called the anchorman's office, where he talked to a woman named Nancy who called herself a producer and sounded as if she wasn't quite paying attention. When Hank reminded her that he'd appeared on their broadcast more than once, she replied, "So has everybody else in town." After that Hank was sure that nothing would come of it, but he was ready to tell Judith that he'd done his best.

The next time he saw her, he thought that she looked exceptionally pretty; new wire-rimmed glasses made her brown eyes appear larger and warmer. As they headed for a table in a popular M Street restaurant (a smoke cloud drifted toward them from the bar), Hank looked worriedly at her faraway expression, but when they sat side by side in a damp wooden booth and he felt welcome nudges from her knee, he said at once, "I spoke to one of Reynolds Mund's producers, who sounded quite interested in that thing we talked about."

"This means a lot to me," she said, and when Hank nodded, hoping for a change of subject, she went on, "I know you think I'm overdoing this, but you have to trust my instincts."

"Not at all, not at all," Hank said, and patted her shoulder, feeling dots of warmth on his fingertips.

"I'm very excited about this," she said.

They had white wine and hamburgers and Hank was surprised when, halfway through, Judith suggested that they go to her apartment for coffee—where they could talk without smoke getting into their eyes. She waved her hand demonstratively as another gray puff surrounded them. Then, as they got into a beaten taxicab with one semiflat tire, Hank watched her skirt slide up and felt, for the first time that night, a stirring. He was not even annoyed when the driver announced that he needed to stop at a filling station to buy gas and inflate his tire.

. . .

THIS WAS HANK's first visit to her place. The lobby had a marble floor that was not clean; there were stains on the wall, and next to the elevators, a sand-filled ashtray overflowed with the filters of cigarettes. But it was one of those early twentieth–century buildings that promised thick walls and views of the federal city, and from Judith's seventh floor you could see over the Potomac. The Monument was a hooded shadow, red eyes glowing, and the silver tubes of airplanes glided behind it and over the river.

"I don't often ask people up," she said.

"I feel honored," Hank replied, and she looked at him sharply.

Her walls were covered by Matisse cutouts, the Washington version of Steinberg's New York, and a photograph of Judith with a few other *Law Review* people. That was taken about the time (it now seemed long ago) when Hank's congressman had quit and Hank had gone to the Institute. A corner was for exercise; a NordicTrack stood there, a moist towel draped across one of the poles.

When Judith went into her small kitchen to make coffee, Hank snooped: he looked at the splintered coffee table, which held a fresh copy of *Runner's World* alongside law journals and *Elle*, and at the fiction of Joyce Carol Oates collected in one bookcase. In the bathroom (he looked for a lock on the door and could not find one) he found six shampoo bottles lined up along the wall of the bathtub; three pink-handled razors; aspirin and contact lens fluid (he hadn't known she sometimes wore them); and, hanging from the shower curtain bar, a pair of panties with a small bloodstain in the crotch. He blushed at his nearness to another life and washed his hands carefully, using the scented liquid soap in a half-filled flask that lay sideways on the edge of the sink.

When he returned to the living room, it was darker. The light that had lit the hallway was dark, and the light from the kitchen was gone; he could see the blue flame of the burner under the kettle. He stumbled over a small stool and made his way back to the sofa.

"My house is such a mess," she said softly. "I'm so busy."

"Mine is worse."

"But mine is bad," she said, and then issued a command: "Sit."

After this sudden descent into darkness, Judith produced a tray with coffee, mugs that advertised Harvard Law, and a half-finished bag of Pepperidge Farm cookies. As she sat beside him, a knee once more touched his, and he thought, heart speeding up, that it would happen! He felt a little panicked. He feared flaccidity; her bony legs might not excite him. Perhaps she was more accustomed to people like herself, thirty-year-olds who worked out and ran miles. He pinched a roll of fat around his stomach.

"What I've always wanted in someone," he heard himself saying, "was a person who interested me in a physical way but could talk about the stuff I do."

"I do like you, Hank," she said. "I work with such sharks all day."

She put her hand on his thigh, and Hank reciprocated at once. Hers felt softer than he'd thought it would. She pulled off her panty hose, which then lay in a silky puddle.

"It's like I've known you for a long time," she said.

"Me too," he said, kicking off his shoes.

He hoped that he understood her. When a woman actually *let* him, it was almost as if another person were doing the deed—the zippers, the surrender—as if a dream were taking over and carrying him thrillingly along.

"I do really appreciate what you've done!" Judith said suddenly, clapping her hands. She got up, bare-legged, and started to pace. "I want you to tell me again what that producer said."

It was like a cross-examination, these repetitions, and before Hank could reply, Judith said, "I'm not sure what to say if they call me." She turned on a light, making Hank squint, sounding worried now. "Those people aren't all that bright. Don't you think she'd call some-one else if they were going to do a story? Maybe Pete Thingeld?"

"I'm sure they'll be thorough," Hank said, glancing at her tense neck. "I'm sure that's what it is."

"Maybe no one will care," Judith said, stopping as she paced to stare intently at Hank. "Then what will we do?"

"I could try to call someone else," Hank said, quick to agree with everything she was saying. "I know some reporters."

"I appreciate," she said, "the way you take this seriously. Not everyone would. Maybe you don't. Do you?"

Hank looked at Judith as tenderly as he could, standing to join her. From the window he could see that a pale mist had settled about the tip of the Monument. In a while Judith turned off the lights, just as she had before, and they sat down again. This time she leaned against him, her hair tickling his cheek. When Hank kissed her, after a silent interval, he was surprised at the size and strength of her tongue. This hadn't happened before! By the time Judith stood to take off more clothing, Hank's eyes had gotten used to the darkness, and he found that he was thinking not only of Judith but of Wendy Lullabay, the actress on *Perfect Fit*, whose body was not nearly so lean as Judith's.

"I think Cuomo is going to win it," Judith said, sitting back as if to catch her breath. "I really do."

"I don't know," Hank said, wondering how that subject came up, thinking that Judith's undergarments were glowing in the darkness and that her legs were beautiful.

"You should volunteer," she said. "Maybe for Dukakis. I met him once in Cambridge."

"Yeah, maybe I should," Hank said, his hand alighting on Judith's bare upper leg.

"You think Reagan's going to pardon those terrible people?" she asked as Hank contemplated the intensity of his stirring rather than a scandal, something about Iran and Nicaragua that he barely understood.

"Maybe," he said, trying to follow her thoughts.

Then, when he felt the time was right, Hank himself took off everything but his Jockey shorts, and then those, a little giddy in his new costume that matched Judith's outfit exactly. In the weeks before Thanksgiving, he thought, this was indeed something to be thankful for. He could not believe his good fortune and then, as he excitedly embraced her on the couch, he thought that he would explode. In seconds, against his determined will, he did. "Sorry," he said, thankful only that the darkness made his body-length blush invisible.

"Don't be," she replied in a tone he could not quite interpret. "Maybe someday we can try again."

NINE

On a bright November afternoon Charles Dingleman strolled through Dumbarton Oaks. He sat on a stone bench, inches from a fresh deposit of birdshit, and thought about his conversation with Skip Haine, which had taken place in Skip's little office down a long inner corridor inside the Old Executive Office Building. Skip had been full of apologies for an unexpected delay, but he'd wanted to assure Charlie that it was no one's fault. Skip had wavy blond hair and a face like a fresh shower. He was a Californian, he told Charlie, and he referred to Ronald Reagan as the governor, pointing to a photograph of himself with Reagan's arm on his shoulder. "I know you want to serve him too, sir," Skip Haine said, and Charlie told him not to say sir.

Skip Haine made repeated references to Fred Hykler, Charlie's best friend on the Hill, and said that everyone, especially Fred, wanted to help. But they also needed to be sure that there was no bad stuff, as he put it, hanging in Charlie's closet—"and to be frank, sir, we've heard some stuff; the FBI has heard some stuff."

"There is no stuff, as you put it," Charlie said to Skip Haine, making himself yawn as if he were bored with the very idea. But he felt humiliated by the thought of people prying into his life and by talking about "bad stuff" with people half his age. It wasn't worth it, he told himself; he'd had enough. Yet when he imagined himself arriving at the White House or the crenellated building where Skip worked, he knew that for him it was worth it. "No stuff, Skip," he said again.

"We hope not, sir, and we hope to have you on board real quick," Skip said, and offered Charlie his almost dainty hand, which Charlie shook heartily.

But later, when Charlie sat and stared at the grounds of Dumbarton Oaks, he considered the inflection of that "we hope not" and had the sensation that his life was now on a path no longer requiring his presence.

Charlie watched squirrels race into trees and leaves descend in twirls. A few young mothers with strollers, occasionally with another child clinging, made their way, and so did men in business suits whose fixed expressions revealed that they had no destination. He saw a woman in a red wool coat and recognized her as the widow of a celebrated journalist, a man who'd known just about everyone. The journalist a few years ago had fallen dead in a hotel room in Bangkok, in the midst of composing a news analysis (and completing, it was rumored, a dalliance), and within weeks of his large funeral (hundreds had shown up at the Washington Cathedral; the bishop had presided), his widow disappeared, as if she had died too. As Charlie exchanged nods with her, he could remember neither her name nor when he'd met her. She kept heading toward him and a few moments later sat on his stone bench.

"Nice to see you," she said, folding her small hands in the lap of her red coat and raising her face toward the sun.

"Nice to see you too, ma'am," Charlie said, looking around as if the park were his, pleased that she seemed to know him. "We should enjoy these days while we can."

"Yes, indeed," the journalist's widow said. "Our town is blessed with its fall weather."

"We pay for it in the summer," Charlie replied uneasily, for this conversation reminded him of hundreds of colloquies that he'd had with constituents.

She was, he guessed, in her early seventies, the same generation as Pete Thingeld. Her mouth was slanted, a grimace of apprehension, and she twisted a piece of tissue, tearing it into shreds that she balled up and stuffed into her coat pocket. When one fragment got away and floated to earth, a large brown squirrel with torn fur dashed out and seized it.

"Little buggers will eat anything," the woman said, shifting about on the stone bench.

Charlie remembered that her name was Rose and that he'd met her years ago at a reception at the Italian embassy on Sixteenth Street: her husband, he recalled, had looked at him shrewdly, as if he might stumble upon an observation Charlie had yet to make. When it was clear that Charlie had nothing to contribute to the journalist's written life, they lunged for the food table with its spread of sausage and fruits and did not speak again that evening. That had been during Charlie's first term, and he remembered turning to his wife and telling her that he, a freshman congressman, might be quoted by an important journalist. It never happened. They rarely ran into one another after that; Charlie with his background was not one of their crowd.

"Do you know who I am?" the woman on the bench asked, sounding almost childlike. "Or am I someone you vaguely recognize and are too embarrassed to ask?"

"Of course I know you," Charlie replied.

"The truth is that I don't know who you are," she said. "I can't for the life of me remember your name."

Charlie, who wished this conversation had never begun, identified himself while the squirrel with torn fur darted past them, inches from their feet, chasing a smaller gray squirrel.

"These days," the widow went on, "I sometimes go for a week without having a real conversation. They are still very nice to me at the grocery and the cleaners, but the bookstore changed hands. It's been a while since I've gotten an invitation to anything."

Charlie saw the anger in her small blue eyes. Her lips were nearly invisible, and a short gray hair grew from a mole on her chin. Dear lady, he thought, why does it still matter so? When he'd first come to Washington, he wondered about the city's old men, many of whom looked the same: thin white hair and nowhere to go during the day. He was sure that by the time he got to be as old as that, he'd no longer care; he might move back to Pennsylvania and practice law. But this no longer seemed realistic. A decade later, at forty-eight, Charlie wanted more than ever to be part of it. It was why Skip Haine mattered so—why it was worth it.

"You know what I mean," the journalist's widow said to Charlie, as if she'd read his mind, and he realized that he hadn't answered her.

"I do know, ma'am," he said politely, and took one of her small, cold hands between his two large ones and squeezed it gently. The gesture seemed to puzzle her, and she stared at her hand as if the fingers had been lost and then found. She smiled at Charlie.

As Charlie left the park with its dormant fountains and tough birds (soon he was going eastward on P Street), he began to feel as if something unpleasant was about to happen. He was familiar with vague worries and knew that he became most apprehensive when his hopes were highest; he used to avoid sidewalk cracks just before an election. But he also knew how lives went awry in Washington.

Coming toward him was a boy who looked like his son, tall with red-brown hair, though of course it could not be him: Chas was twenty-four and working with some computer thing in California. Nor had he ever looked like this kid who, Charlie now saw, had dull eyes and a lot of acne. His daughter, Jessica, who was twenty-two and a senior at Tufts, had been asking for money to buy a used car, and he'd meant to send her some. No doubt the FBI knew lots more about him than his children did, and perhaps at this moment agents were handing supplementary files to Skip Haine, a report that would include details of the terrible squabbles he'd had with Abigail (or perhaps Eve, with whom he fought in a different, colder way).

Abigail had not liked being a congressman's wife. From the start she had hated the receptions and going to the district and being forced to smile at constituents, many of whom would never vote for Charlie. Often, as they drove up or down Route 15, Abigail would say, "I really don't know why I'm there," speaking in a voice that he dreaded, for there was no escape from the car.

"I like being with you," he'd reply, trying to be lighthearted.

"I do nothing, Charlie. I know you get angry when I call myself a prop, but you can't deny that that's exactly what I am."

"I deny it. You're my partner."

"I'm your prop," she would say, sometimes adding, "A prop you fuck."

"You do not have to do all this," he would say. "You can stay home."

"I know what happens when a congressman's wife stays home," she would reply.

"It's even worse when you're miserable," Charlie would say.

"You sometimes seem to be accusing me of being miserable on purpose," Abigail would say, her face becoming red to the roots of her brown-red hair, the words almost always the same, as if their squabbles were scripted.

Abigail didn't go to a bill-signing ceremony (their first invitation, in the summer of 1981, to the Reagan White House) because she had nothing to wear. She called Charlie two hours before the event, and Charlie kicked a chair that some believed had historical value, perhaps having been used by John Quincy Adams. On the way to cocktail parties she would cry and even threaten to jump from the car. When they arrived, she would tug at his sleeve, her eyes moist, and tell him that she was leaving—that no one would miss her anyway. Now and then she would disappear into the night, sometimes abandoning him in mid-conversation, frightening him with the speed of her vanishings. He would be fearful not only of the moment but of their future; he knew, while trying not to know, that these were not just squabbles.

"You embarrassed me," he would say in his distress when he'd caught up with her, usually hours later. "You really scared me." One night in McLean she lay on the floor and shrieked, "I'm useless!" Charlie, not knowing what to say or how to say it, went back to his office. He drove slowly along the Potomac and across the Memorial Bridge, stopping at the not-quite-Grecian memorials, not finding in the face of Lincoln or the words of Jefferson the comfort that was promised. When he got to his office, admiring for just an instant the gold letters of his name on the door, he called home and told Abigail he was spending the night on his couch, and when she hung up he felt, most of all, relief.

When Charlie thought about this years later, he would think that it was Abigail's fault, that she had pushed him away. He would also feel sentimental about their life together—half of his life—and after they had gone separate ways he began to understand what had made her unhappy. One night when he watched Johnny Carson and Eve still had not come home, he turned and spoke out loud, as if to Abigail. "Sorry," he said.

. . .

HAVING REACHED Sixteenth Street without paying attention to where he was, Charlie turned south, passed the Soviet embassy (the White House glimmered from the short distance), and then turned west to his office. Everyone seemed to have heard that he was getting a job in the White House, and while it was always difficult to read the expressions of lawyers, he sensed that no one was sorry to say good-bye. Charlie had never belonged. He had not billed as many hours as the others, his litigation record was mediocre, and he rarely signed up top clients. On those rare weekends that he'd gone in to work, he would find a cadre of associates whose determination frightened him; they wore running shoes and blue jeans and sweat-shirts that carried the brand names of their colleges. Sometimes on Sunday afternoons they'd watch the bright television in the confer-ence room and catch glimpses of the firm's partners on the forty-three-yard line, clapping their mittens to urge the Redskins on. Charlie stayed away from the Redskins too.

He was halfway down the corridor when Tonya, the secretary he shared with an associate, removed her headset. "You have lots of calls this morning, Congressman," she said.

"You make that sound scary," Charlie replied, smiling. But he saw that she looked worried and that all the messages were from some-one who worked at a local television station, which made him a little worried too.

TEN

(Thanksgiving Ceremonies)

Hank Morriday dreaded Thanksgiving, which he had to spend in Paterson, New Jersey, where his father, a retired school-teacher, lived alone, and in the Philadelphia suburbs, where his mother lived with his stepfather, who owned a men's clothing store. None of these relatives, he was sure, had the slightest interest in the welfare system or the working poor or an equitable society. It was no better at the Institute, where Hank was definitely not cheered up by hearing that Michael Dukakis was going to speak at the annual dinner. That only reminded him that he didn't know Mike, as he was called by everyone who did know him.

Other things were getting to Hank as the grim holidays approached. He wished that he hadn't made that telephone call for Judith Grust, even if nothing ever came of it; he wasn't sure that he trusted Judith's powers of observation. He was perhaps more troubled by his anatomical treachery at the very moment that Judith had been willing—more than willing, actually disrobed, her legs about to part. At the same time Hank was bothered by an event of absolutely no significance, although he could not stop thinking about it.

Now and then Hank and the people he knew would talk about the remarkable fact that the great majority of Washington's population was of African descent and that they themselves, being white, knew very few people of the other color. "I feel as if I'm being cut off from so much," Hank sometimes remarked mournfully, usually adding, "It's as if we're living in half a city." He supposed that his work suffered from the fact that he had nothing to do with the people he wrote about, but what he hated to admit to himself was that it made him uncomfortable to be around black people. He chose to blame this on black people, who seemed to be uncomfortable around him.

What had happened was this: He had gone to Fourteenth Street to buy new shoes, a pair of tasseled loafers just like the scuffed ones he was about to give up on, and he remembered the moment exactly because he'd noticed the Monument, its top whiter in bright sunlight, and he'd also been thinking about those new shoes, for which he'd decided to spend as much as one hundred dollars, if that was what it took. He pictured his newly shod foot pressing the accelerator of his Beemer, and this particular focus may have been why he didn't see the two young men, both wearing hooded Redskins sweatshirts, who brushed him as they passed.

"Hey, man, watch where you going," the taller one said, giving Hank a hard look. He might have been sixteen.

"Sorry," Hank replied, not meeting the stare he got.

"Yeah, you sorry, motherfucker," the second youth, who was perhaps fourteen, said.

They pushed Hank, who fell to his knees, surprised by the shove and at being the center of attention (others nearby backed off, as if he had something contagious). For a moment Hank thought that the two young men—boys—were going to beat him; his body tensed as if for a blow, but they shrugged and walked away laughing with something of a swagger. A matronly woman with short white hair stopped as he pushed himself up from the pavement and brushed his knees. "Did they hurt you?" she asked. When he said that he was all right, not quite sure what had just happened, he saw fiery hatred in her eyes. "People can't live in this city anymore," she said. She shook her head, and others who had stopped to watch shook their heads too. Hank stared at the glare off the Monument and felt for a moment as if he were not entirely there, as if he were nearly imperceptible, a transit of Venus. Clusters of people passed, mostly people with dark skin who made him uncomfortable; he wanted to run after the two young men and say, "Hey, man, talk to me," although he had nothing in particular to tell them.

. . .

CHARLIE DINGLEMAN spent Thanksgiving Day by himself. Eve had gone to visit her family in Winston-Salem, or so she said, and his children were with their mother in McLean. He ate frozen food—two not-bad Stouffer's dinners—and on Friday he took Chas and Jessica to a seafood restaurant in Bethesda. While they ate, Charlie learned that someone named James, who worked in the same real estate office as Abigail, had come for Thanksgiving; that Abigail had remodeled the kitchen (she was doing really well); and that they'd seen several neighbors whose names Charlie had almost forgotten. All this was disclosed between tormented silences.

"Dad, you're looking great," Chas said several times, enough to make Charlie worry.

Chas and Jessica looked more like Abigail than Charlie remembered, with the same freckled noses and reddish hair; Jessica seemed to have gotten taller and prettier, and she had her mother's borderline reckless smile. They talked about the White House job, and several times Jessica said, "Dad, it's just so perfect for you," and

Chas added, "Absolutely perfect." Charlie hoped that they were proud of him, but the White House had been spookily silent again and Charlie, although he did not want to think about it, knew how things could go wrong. The insane telephone call from that airhead television lady was one thing that worried him. As they chattered on—Chas talked about computers and California; Jessica wondered what she'd do after graduating from Tufts—Charlie found himself thinking about Abigail. Holiday sentiment, he thought, and yet why not telephone, just to ask how things were and talk about the children? What could be more natural? After the meal the three of them stood outside, facing Wisconsin Avenue, and took too long to say good-bye before Chas and Jessica got into the Chevy they'd rented for their short stay and Charlie in his Olds Cutlass headed back to Georgetown.

．．．

TERESA MARACOPULOS and Martin Himmelschaft drove to her parents' home in the village of Horseheads, on the outskirts of Elmira. She enjoyed the drive north, the snow on the mountains, swerving once to avoid a dog-sized woodchuck outside Gettysburg. On one telephone pole south of Williamsport was a faded DINGLE-MAN FOR C NGRESS poster, the O shot out by a hunter's bullet.

Teresa knew that Martin found it hard to be with her family, although he could talk about shotguns with her father and throw around a football with her younger brother. "I wish they wouldn't keep asking if Jewish people celebrated Thanksgiving," Martin had said every year. Teresa too found it a strain to follow conversations that she'd heard all her life. Her father, who managed a plumbing supply house in Elmira and wore shirts the color of potato skins, had shot a ten-point buck this year, and as he explained how he'd tracked him for hours and waited in a tree, Teresa realized that she'd not heard a word, although she was worrying that he'd put on too much weight, the way his belly hung down. Nor was she listening when her mother complained that she had to drive to Rochester to find decent shopping or when her brother kept asking, "How're Ron and Nancy?" Her mother sometimes leaned her way and asked, "So *what* is it that this Big Tooth place does?" When Teresa replied that they tried to help unfortunate people, no one quite believed her. Nor did anyone believe Martin when he said that he didn't mind working in a place with a lot of black people.

Teresa knew that her work friends would be baffled by the crèche in the Maracopulos front yard, by the souvenir plates from Athens, by Teresa's grandmother, who spoke with a comical accent, and by her cousin Leo, who had spent nine months in jail for driving a car that he'd borrowed from someone he'd never met. She also knew that her family would never understand why she enjoyed being at a place like Big Tooth. What, for instance, had possessed her to act like a chauffeur for Reynolds Mund, who, she had to admit, had then behaved in a strange way? Even worse, why had she gone into his house? When she compared Reynolds Mund to her father, it was as if the planet were divided not only by nations and races but by something more profound.

On the Friday after Thanksgiving, as Hank Morriday and his father silently watched a football game and Charlie Dingleman had dinner with his grown-up children, Teresa took Martin to the Arnot Mall, covered with pine and red ribbon, and they wandered from store to store—the Gap, Mr. Panosian's, and Tape World. They ran into one of Teresa's high school classmates, a former track star who had slightly mismatched dark eyes and whose girlfriend, Teresa remembered, had been killed in a car crash on the night of the prom. Afterward Teresa hugged Martin. In Washington he never quite belonged; even at the Big Tooth Christmas party, where other spouses looked as if they were having fun, Martin stood in a corner looking bored and sulky. But up here he felt so solid and understanding. She knew that Martin loved her desperately, the way he sometimes just stared at her large breasts and dainty nipples. That night, as the Maracopulos family downstairs sprawled in front of the television and watched a movie about a family homecoming, Teresa climbed on top of Martin and rocked back and forth, moaning to excite him and promising herself that she'd behave.

ELEVEN

By early December, when the air was chilly and wet and fili-
grees of tinsel crisscrossed the city, the cheerful Skip Haine called
Charlie to say again that everyone was looking forward to his board-
ing the mother ship; they still felt—and Skip reminded Charlie that
he had many enthusiastic supporters—that Charlie was a perfect
choice because of his experience and because most people seemed
to like him. This made Charlie happy, as it did when a newspaper
column mentioned him in connection with possible White House
"holdovers." Then he'd think about the people who didn't like
him—those turncoats in Pennsylvania—and the Sierra Club types
who made fun of his work for the Fisheries Management subcommittee, and he'd actually worry about the telephone calls from that
television person. For a while the producer lady seemed to have forgotten him, but there she was again. Tonya's message slip read,
"Call Nancy (producer for Reynolds Mund). Urgent."

When he thought about Nancy the producer, he rocked in his
chair and stared at a pile of documents, all having to do with matters
that he was responsible for: a zoning dispute in Montgomery
County, where a defense contractor wanted its new laboratory to
conduct unspecified research with stray cats; a consulting firm's tax
problem (it hadn't paid any); the mineral rights case that he'd asked
Judith Grust to help with and which had returned to his desk in an
unmarked folder. Charlie hoped that the television person's calls

were about a case, but he knew better: that they had something to do with the White House job—no doubt some leftover scurrility from his last campaign. He was sure that someone was out to get him, although he couldn't imagine who or why. After all, the Democrats had defeated him; a former D.A. with a thumb-sized mustache had taken his seat in Congress along with the things that Charlie missed the most—the cheap haircuts, the saunas and pool, his own staff, the stationery.

Charlie just hated this, because he knew that sooner or later he'd have to call back and that nothing good would come of it. He finally did so at lunchtime, hoping to show goodwill while avoiding an actual conversation. But his attempt at telephonic duplicity failed; Nancy the producer was eating a sandwich at her desk.

"Hi!" she said sweetly and enthusiastically. "Thanks for getting back to me."

"Glad to help," Charlie said in a jovial tone.

She only had a few questions, and if he didn't mind, she'd just plug in her tape recorder. To Charlie's surprise, though, her questions were not about his losing race or even any of his clients, but about something else—something so preposterous that he had no idea how to respond.

After they were finished—the conversation took less than five minutes—Charlie sat quite motionless, looking at the spines of unread law books, then getting up to stare down at K Street where, on this early December afternoon, the lunchtime crowds were out. For several minutes, after shredding old telephone messages, he stood there, and then he sat again at his desk and called the 456 number to reach Skip Haine. Charlie's face was red when he told Skip that *News at Five* as well as *News at Six* and probably *News at Eleven* just might have a little story about him that was entirely false, and furthermore if they put it on the air, he would sue.

"Stay cool, Congressman," Skip Haine said soothingly.

"It's just a complete insane lie," Charlie said, feeling a shiver through his body.

"I wouldn't worry about it," Skip Haine said. "It sounds to me like a bump in the road and it's rattling the car a bit."

"But I'm in the car and you're not," Charlie said, squeezing the telephone.

"I've watched lots of these cars go by," Skip Haine said. "And if it's not true—and I believe you totally—all you have to do is say it, and then the story goes away. Eventually it does, anyway."

Charlie breathed deeply, gripping the telephone tighter.

"Sometimes it doesn't go away," he said.

"That's true, sometimes it doesn't," Skip Haine agreed.

Charlie went home in the late afternoon. He sat in the kitchen and listened to the answering machine: Eve had called to say that she'd be late and perhaps would spend the night with a girlfriend. Charlie kicked at the refrigerator, and as he walked around the house (up and down the stairs three times), he had to wonder again about their marriage. Instants after she climbed into bed, she'd fall asleep; during the night, when they bumped into each other, she would whisper, "I'm just too tired, sweetheart. Let's do this tomorrow," but she rarely kept that promise. When they talked, it was usually Eve asking about the law. As Charlie paced, sometimes nervously clapping his hands together, he saw that the bright Cabestan rug was not quite flat and that a slightly moist copy of *Vogue* was on the bathroom floor. The ficus in the corner of the living room had at last perished and in death had turned dark brown. The mail was in a pile, much of it unopened. Charlie knew that bills were unpaid and that his credit rating might be skidding. For a few minutes he looked through a catalogue that sold spying devices and thought about how he might use a camera the size of a postage stamp. He thought of how Eve's skin sometimes appeared translucent and of how she looked at him past her long, sharp nose. Then he felt a spasm of unexpected jealousy.

At five o'clock Charlie lay on the bed and watched the friendly face of Reynolds Mund go through the day's news: a drive-by shooting in Southeast, visits to Iowa by five Democrats who were running for president, and a scandal about a larcenous Santa Claus. Then almost abruptly, with a worried look, the popular anchorman said that "questions have been raised about a possible White House appointment." Mund spoke while the screen showed the exterior of the Thingeld, Pine building and bunches of people, some with Christmas shopping bags, walking by; then he mentioned Charlie's name. There were, the anchorman said, reports of "sexual harassment in the inner sanctum of the legal establishment," and a "source confirmed that former congressman Dingleman was receiving treatment." Charlie saw his own face—an official photograph from four years ago—and as his face expanded to fill the television screen, he thought that it looked a little scary, the face of someone who might enjoy experimenting with stray cats. Then Mund turned to his pretty coanchor, who looked distressed at the news about Charlie, shook her long, yellow-streaked hair with disapproval, and with a dazzling smile changed the subject.

. . .

THE NEXT MORNING, in the few hours that Charlie spent at Thingeld, Pine, eyes were averted. Charlie wanted to shake everyone and make them swear they did not believe it. But he knew that they were ready to believe every word; he also knew that he would have been all too willing to believe such things about any one of them.

Charlie had not lost his political skills. After all, he'd been through hard times before, and he knew that Skip Haine was right—that even the worst moments did not last. In fact Skip had called Charlie right after the broadcast and told him that he still had the full support of everyone at the White House. When Charlie telephoned Fred Hykler to say there was no truth to the story—that it was someone's fantasy—Charlie's best friend in Congress said that he too believed him utterly. When Charlie said that he was considering a lawsuit, Hykler paused for an instant and said, "It makes you wonder where those people get these stories from."

"Somebody had it in for me," Charlie assured him.

"Everybody in Washington has it in for somebody," Fred said. "That's why we all got to be real careful what we do."

In the silence that followed this folksy, lugubrious analysis, Charlie realized that Fred from this point on wanted little to do with him.

"I didn't do anything," Charlie said.

"*I* know that," Fred said, "and *you* know it. But that's not always enough."

Charlie took several deep breaths and supposed that if worse came to worst and the offer was withdrawn, he'd survive. After all, people said that the Republicans were going to lose the White House next November, and he'd be giving up a pretty good income for a one-year job. When he stepped out of his office to head to the bathroom, Tonya gave him a tender smile and did not avert her eyes. He was enormously grateful when she said, "That's a lot of shit they're saying, Mr. Dingleman," and his impulse was to embrace her. Although there were not many other signs of support, Charlie imagined that was because no one watched the local news. So, he told himself, to hell with it.

Charlie became so intent on adopting this new perspective that he didn't hear the muffled *tap, tap* on his door and did not look up until it opened slightly and he saw the pale face of Anthony "Pete" Thingeld, who smiled weakly. A moment later the founding partner and former deputy attorney general closed the door, a sign that what he had to say was confidential.

"Charlie, I fear that the fault may lie with me," Thingeld said, blinking his watery eyes, brushing flecks of invisible dust from the front of his dark gray pinstriped suit.

"What do you mean, Pete?" Charlie asked.

"I mean that the assurances I gave one of our associates about you," Thingeld said, scratching an ear from which a clump of white hair grew, "may have been transformed into something malign."

Charlie sat up straight. "I'm not sure," he said, "that I follow you," although Charlie was following perfectly.

"You know my feeling that small lies are the lubricant of civilization," Thingeld said. "I want to be clear about this: it's not vicious, harmful, self-serving lies that I mean, but small lies—the ones that preserve commerce and civility."

Charlie nodded, listening carefully to what the senior partner was saying: that he had improvised a little—had added a detail or so to fill out a small fib he'd told to calm down Judith Grust. But he feared that he may have added too much; he could not recall precisely what he'd said.

"So it could be my doing," Thingeld concluded, a sorrowful whisper overtaking his words. "I just wanted to help smooth things out."

"You actually told someone I was being treated for a sexual *disorder*?" Charlie said calmly, although his heart was beating at high speed. "I thought you told her I was just feeling, you know, *stress*. That's what I thought. This is very bad for me, Pete."

Thingeld looked embarrassed at hearing it phrased in that way. Charlie stood up and walked over to the window and tried to imagine what the founding partner might have said to Judith Grust.

"Jesus Christ," Charlie said.

"I was trying to protect you," Thingeld said a little plaintively. "These women around here, some of them are absolutely crazy. You look at their tight little asses and perky tits and they complain. You touch them the wrong way and you're done for. I'll tell you, there was a time when these girls behaved themselves, but now . . ." Thingeld's voice became a little wistful. "The point is, Charlie, that I chose the lesser of two evils."

Charlie looked intently at the older partner and felt, for a moment, sorry for his discomfort.

"Or what I thought was the lesser," Thingeld added, his eyes cast down.

"Did you by any chance say precisely what sort of problem I had?" Charlie asked.

"I would never have done that—never violated privilege," the founding partner replied, with a shocked expression.

TWELVE

Teresa Maracopulos hadn't talked about her excursion with the anchorman—not even to Candy Romulade, her best work friend. Not that there was much to tell, but in retrospect it had been pretty strange, almost from the moment when he'd asked with a mock-pleading grin if she wouldn't mind taking a tiny little detour; he needed to pick up something at home. It wouldn't take long, he'd assured her, and then they could hop right over to the television station. As Teresa drove, he'd kept muttering something she could not quite hear. The first few times she'd asked him to repeat it, but when she still could not make out the words, she'd stopped asking.

Across the Maryland line, with its speed bumps and oversized trees, Teresa saw an au pair girl yanking a little boy's arm, the plumbing-and-heating vans, and the station wagons piloted by young mothers with fixed expressions. When she saw the anchorman's big white clapboard house, she thought about her own cramped quarters in a mean part of town.

For a moment she felt as if someone were watching her and then as if she were watching herself. "It's not modest, but it's mine," the anchorman said with a grin, in a way that suggested he had said the same thing many times before. Teresa admired the proportions of the house and supposed that it seemed larger inside because there was almost no furniture. It was as if no one quite lived there; the floor of the living room was dusty, and a dried trail of mouse turds led to an equally bare kitchen, where not even a coffee cup was visible. Arranged on a table in the dining room was a collection of awards: metal figures holding globes and basketballs, celebratory plaques. One door in the dining room was secured with a padlock.

"It's a wonderful house," Teresa said. "Why is that door locked?"

The anchorman nodded and smiled his gentle smile, one in which his slightly crooked nose moved and crinkles spread out from his eyes; it was the smile that viewers saw when he bantered with his news team—the weatherman who did tap dances with a pointer, the bellowing sports reporter who had once pitched for the Washington Senators, and his coanchor, the one with the yellow-streaked hair.

"Good question," he said.

Teresa thought hard about what to say next, wanting more than anything to sound wise, to impress him. The anchorman though seemed to be looking at her with puzzled amusement, and she also noticed for the first time a fogginess in his eyes.

"But I mean, is it a secret?" she asked.

"You're a very perceptive person, Tracy," he said. "I like that."

"Teresa," she replied, and the anchorman nodded.

"It was kind of you to drive me here," he added.

Because she had felt a draft, Teresa had kept her coat on. When she wrapped her arms around herself, the anchorman smiled with sympathy. She wondered again about the locked door and imagined a movie plot—that he kept someone prisoner in there. She shivered.

"It's a little chilly," he said. "I'm not here often enough."

Teresa looked closely at him and believed that sadness lay behind his merry eyes.

"Such a beautiful house, it's a shame," she said.

The anchorman chuckled and said, "I know what you're thinking. You're thinking, 'Why isn't there a Mrs. Mund? Why does he have to live in this beautiful house all by himself?' Isn't that so?"

"I can't deny that it occurred to me," Teresa replied, "but it's none of my business."

"And you're thinking that something mysterious is in that room."

"Well, I'm curious."

"Those are good questions," the anchorman said. "You'd make a good correspondent."

"So?" Teresa asked.

But he seemed by then to have forgotten what he'd said, and he walked to the kitchen, offering to make coffee, apologizing for having only Taster's Choice, finding two cups in an otherwise empty cabinet. Teresa saw flat-looking beams of light from the late sun and thought that Martin might be trying to call her; he often phoned Big Tooth to see when she'd be done and then to make plans for the evening—what video to rent perhaps.

"I can't stay long," she said, looking at her watch. "Also didn't you say you had to get to work?"

"Your husband is probably the jealous sort," he said.

Was he being sarcastic? You couldn't tell with him.

"Is there a place to sit?" she asked, knowing that she had just sounded annoyed. "I mean," she added, this time smiling a little flirtatiously, "do people just stand here? Also my husband doesn't know where I am."

The anchorman looked at Teresa pityingly.

"All right, I'll show you," he said, as if she'd been demanding something, and then he went to the locked door. "I know you're very curious."

The padlock made a very loud snap when he opened it.

"It's no big deal," he said, "but I don't want strangers walking in."

He made a gesture for her to follow. Teresa hesitated because he was making her nervous. Even from a distance she could see through the doorway that the walls in the other room were covered with photographs; when she got closer she saw that all of them had been signed by their subjects. Halogen lights hung from the ceiling; a television screen was cut into a wall.

"Sit wherever you want," the anchorman told her, pointing to four chairs with rush seats.

"This is really amazing," Teresa said after she'd looked around for a couple of minutes.

"It's no big deal," the anchorman said again. "It's my private gallery."

"I really love it," Teresa said, regarding the images of famous people that he'd met, people like the three Kennedy brothers and Mickey Mantle and Elizabeth Taylor, a Beatle and many Redskins and Hubert Humphrey, a pope, and someone named Chet Huntley, who had misspelled the anchorman's name.

"I love it too," he said, and smiled his happiest smile.

"Wow," she said.

Teresa knew that people like Reynolds Mund made lots of money, but she'd never thought about how they spent it. She wondered if the anchorman would come on to her; his moods seemed so changeable that she didn't know what to expect. The next time she looked at him, he turned away, as if he were embarrassed.

"Your life must be so exciting," Teresa said, and wished that she didn't keep sounding so silly and immature.

"I like being at the center of the action," he replied, and his smile was accompanied by a sad droop in his mouth.

Then, to Teresa's surprise, the anchorman began to speak angrily about people—horrible people, it turned out—who worked at the television station, and he pointed to photographs of the other news regulars, the "team," with crayon marks scratched almost angrily across their grinning faces. "They hate me," he told her. "They think I'm an idiot. And they're jealous." He looked at the faces on his walls and said, "Every time I see my gallery, I know how it ends for all of us." He looked both melancholy and wise as he said this, and Teresa wondered again if he was going to do something sexual and what she would do if he did. She imagined a naked man's body with that locally famous head attached to it.

The anchorman turned a switch and the television screen went bright; he seemed briefly to forget that she was even there as they watched moving images of people that he'd interviewed and then events, a few from before his time—the Hindenburg caught fire— and some recent ones, such as an airplane that fell into the Potomac. At first the anchorman was silent. Then he said, "It's best when you can actually *make* news molecules." He looked warmly into her eyes as Teresa felt another draft and made sure that her wool coat was buttoned up. She had no idea what he was talking about. Later, after she had dropped him off at the television station in Tenleytown, as she was driving east on Military Road, the darkness of Rock Creek Park coming on quite suddenly, Teresa realized that "news molecules" were the words that he'd been muttering earlier.

THIRTEEN

CHARLES DINGLEMAN contacted Big Tooth even before the sunny Skip Haine stopped returning his calls. He spoke to the only partner he knew, the former senator, who had the slow, deep voice of a country song and assured Charlie that just as people with serious illnesses consulted doctors, people with terrible reputations consulted places like Big Tooth. In this soothing voice (the voice that Skip Haine would have in twenty-five years) he told Charlie that they had just the person to manage his troubled affairs. "She's one of the best gals we have," he said. "I want to work with *you*," Charlie protested, invoking what he imagined was the brotherhood of Congress. But the ex-senator only chuckled and said, "When you have one Big Toother working for you, you have all the Big Teeth on your team." Then he added, "Charlie, believe me, you can't afford me. It's getting so I can't afford myself." At that he giggled.

Charlie didn't think that was funny, not the way things were going, and of course there was nothing that a place like Big Tooth could do about his marriage. A few days earlier Charlie had come home and found Eve going through drawers and closets; she was packing, throwing bundles of clothing into a flexible black three-suiter that belonged to Charlie.

"I can't take it anymore," Eve said, looking up at him. "I mean we have nothing in common, and you just go around in your bad mood while I'm trying to start up my life."

"Do you have any idea why I'm in a bad mood?" Charlie asked.

Eve shook her head, and Charlie realized that Eve had never mentioned his problem because she didn't know a thing about it. He also believed that she wouldn't care, which is why he hadn't told her right away.

"We all get in bad moods," she said.

As he watched her pack (now she was gathering up her loose stockings, and she fished a green lace panty, one he'd never seen her wear, from a drawer and tossed it floatingly into the suitcase next to "The River" T-shirt), he thought how different this was from his last separation, when he was forced to do the packing.

"Are you going on a trip?" he asked, after he'd stood there a little longer.

"You're a good guy, Charlie, but it's over," she said. She smiled sweetly and added, "Hey, you've known that for a while."

When she telephoned for a taxi, she had a concentrated look, as if her mind was on nothing else. Then she turned to him and said, "It's not as though I won't ever be back."

Charlie reflected that even if he was not all that fond of Eve anymore, he might have become so again; and when the Diamond cab honked and she gave him a swift hug and looked up at him, her sharp nose tilted, he felt abandoned. He kept shaking his head as his wife walked out (an R Street neighbor, accompanied by a fat collie, stared); he supposed he should have helped with that suitcase, but the taxi driver hopped right to it and Charlie turned away from the window.

A few days later Eve called to say that she had moved into an apartment in Foggy Bottom, that she was sharing it with someone she described as both a "friend" and a "smart classmate" (ageless, genderless), and that it was a good time to figure out what she wanted—and what Charlie wanted too, she was quick to add. But although she'd gone, Charlie sensed that she was hovering about.

Now and then when he came home he would find objects missing: silverware, an embroidered cushion. If Charlie had not felt so miserable about the future, he might have given more thought to Eve's plunder, especially when she took the Cabestan, the centerpiece of the living room. In its place she left a bamboo mat and a note: "Charlie—I was the one who picked this out. What are you doing for Xmas? Hope it's fun! Fondly, E."

. . .

THE PALE CITY was decorated with candy canes and Hermès ties, and on a semichilly morning, with a few snowflakes listlessly circling the trees, Charlie walked west to the yellow brick building that jutted slightly over the sidewalk of K Street near Nineteenth. When he arrived on Big Tooth's floor, he felt at once like a supplicant or worse—like someone being rolled into the operating room with a sheet pulled up to his nose. A Christmas wreath hung close to the firm's symbol, those huge front teeth embedded in the planet Earth. The wraithlike receptionist, who had puffed-up dark hair and sulky bright lips, waited for Charlie to say something; she smirked when he did, and then she buzzed.

"She's in that way," the receptionist said, a finger pointing.

Charlie walked along a corridor and came to a smaller, darker office where he saw Candy Romulade for the first time, her right index finger twisting her dark blond hair. The size of the office made Charlie wonder whether his account was somehow less valuable than others.

His first glimpse of Candy did not reassure him: the lines around her mouth told him of thoughtless boyfriends, the softness under her eyes of sleepless nights, and the brittle darkness of her tan of attempts to escape both. She led him at once to the elevator, down to the street, and into a taxi—"I hate to talk in the office," she said— where they sat for several minutes as a motorcade sped by; Mikhail Gorbachev had come to town for a state visit.

"Big excitement," Candy Romulade said.

"A remarkable moment," Charlie replied.

"Historic," Candy said, looking not at Charlie but at the traffic that had congealed. "Particularly after Andripov."

Wasn't that An*drop*ov? Charlie wondered as Candy sensed his doubts and hurried to establish herself, to tell him that she had worked for Jimmy Carter's first campaign and discovered (she smiled) that she had an unusual talent: she could persuade other people to do horrid chores. She'd organized telephone banks and direct mailings in two Midwestern states, and then she'd worked in the public affairs office of the Federal Trade Commission. A year later she was hired by the White House press office, where she stayed until Big Tooth recruited her. She had been regarded as a catch; her wide-smiling picture appeared in the company's newsletter, which described her as someone who had "years of public affairs experience for public sector clients as well as companies in key industry segments." She did not tell Charlie that because her client list did not grow, she got leftovers from the partners and was consigned to sharing an office with Teresa Maracopulos.

They rode to the Adams Morgan neighborhood and a restaurant where the tables were covered in checkered oilcloth. There was clatter all around: plates of French cooking carried to tilting tables and glasses raised, voices from a lunchtime crowd that did not wear ties; perspiration shone on the face of the fat cashier.

"So talk to me," Candy Romulade said, leaning across the table, her eyes intense, lighting a cigarette, for she had recently gone back to smoking a lot of them.

"It's crazy," Charlie said. "It just came in from left field."

When he raised his right arm and swore that he had no psychiatric problems, none, he couldn't read her expression. When he told her that he believed it had all started because of one person, she leaned toward him, streams of smoke coming from her nostrils; she nibbled on a bread crust and spoke rapidly: "We need to prepare an action plan," Candy said, "and we need to list the options you think you have, from the worst result to the best, and what we have to do to get you there." She took a breath and drew on the cigarette, then: "We work together and believe me, the people at Big Tooth know their business. We don't promise results, but we like to think we get them. We've helped quite a few people like you—people in *much* worse shape."

Charlie did not know what she was talking about, but he detected a rising confidence in her voice that did nothing to encourage him. He also glanced about nervously; although they were not downtown, he still might run into someone he knew.

"You have to remember," Candy Romulade was saying, "that you have a story to tell too and that you can have a lot of people working in your behalf. It's just important to be honest with yourself. We'll be a lot more honest with you than even your best friends will be."

Charlie wished he could pay closer attention, but no matter how he concentrated, a lot of what she said did not make sense. He shrugged this off; for some time he'd had the sensation of hearing a language just a step removed from English. But he also knew that it was important to listen. His fingers gripped his fork when Candy mentioned Big Tooth's fees, which were not so very different from the amounts charged at Thingeld, Pine & Sconce. When their food arrived, Charlie could barely eat his too-red salmon.

· · ·

THE NEXT DAY Candy called Charlie to ask for a list of people who might help him—influential people.

"What would they actually do?" Charlie asked. "I'm still besmirched."

"Well, give me some names—people on the Hill, all around, journalists," Candy said, ignoring his question. "What about your wife?"

"She's very busy with law school."

"I understand," Candy said, as if she heard this sort of thing all the time. "None of this is essential of course. These are just components, as we develop client-specific goals."

Charlie shook his head, and he tried to get Candy to listen to him about Judith Grust.

"I mean, look: someone dropped a dime on me," he said. "Plain and simple."

"That's just the kind of helpful information we like to have" was her response, but she sounded as if she thought Charlie was addled.

Perhaps he was. But there was no other explanation for what had happened to him. People talked—especially in this city, this town, as they called it. Washington was a web of intersecting people, few wishing each other well.

.   .   .

A few days later, Charlie called Fred Hykler, his best friend on the Hill, hoping that his instincts about Fred had been wrong. When Fred did not return the call, his apprehension got the better of him; he rushed the two blocks from his office to the Big Tooth building.

Candy looked up in surprise, and then she scolded him mildly. "Charlie, you should always call first." She pointed to a thin folder with his name on it and then plucked a cigarette from her purse and brought it to crackling life, sending gusts of gray through her nostrils. "I think we're ready to move, but don't be too eager," she told him. "Don't forget, you're damaged goods. You can't unring a bell. So I'm working out a plan I think you'll like—getting people who matter to tell the story of a good man who was treated unfairly. I want them to be outraged! So don't worry. But I just want to run this by the partners."

Charlie was worrying about all of it when she added, "Maybe I'll call that Judith woman you mentioned—Grust? It's a risk, but maybe."

Charlie was feeling almost fearful when the other woman in the office, Teresa Maracopulos, looked at him with curiosity.

"I should have introduced Teresa," Candy said. "She is very close to our favorite local anchorman—you know who, the man who rang the bell."

"Reynolds Mund?" Charlie asked a little stupidly, and then wondered if it was safe to say anything around here. Teresa, he noticed, blushed and then glared at Candy Romulade.

FOURTEEN

In the years that Hank Morriday had struggled with the problems of the down-and-out, Suzanne Smule had thrived with the Soviet Union. Not only was Suzanne far more visible than Hank, she was also a favorite of the Institute's director, Randolph Maintree. Hank found this to be a minor mystery because Suzanne Smule spoke no Russian, had published no monographs, and had never actually visited the place, apart from a weeklong conference in Leningrad, where she had gotten sick from the water. Nor was she especially interested in the Soviet Union. When Soviet citizens stopped by the Institute, Suzanne Smule found them boorish and foul-smelling. They frequently talked Russian, and it annoyed her to be reminded of her linguistic handicap.

Her expert status had been thrust upon her shortly after the Soviet Union's invasion of Afghanistan in 1979, which she had come to refer to as a "fateful December." The television networks and opinion pages had called the Institute, eager to track down an authority on those far-off events, but had found the place deserted for the holidays. The expert on Soviet nationalities was traveling in the Ukraine, the arms specialist was at a conference in Fiji, and the historian who had studied the Communist Bloc for a quarter-century was taking a sabbatical in Berlin. Randolph Maintree, casting about for someone to carry the Institute's banner, nearly gave up until he remembered the stocky, charming woman who'd once been on the staff of the National Security Council. He could not remember why she'd become a Fellow, but he recalled something about a memorable stay in Leningrad, and from that moment he urged people to get in touch with Suzanne Smule, assuring them that she knew a good deal more than a lot of other people. During the following week Suzanne Smule, looking doleful and worried, appeared on several television panels; she was quoted in magazines and newspapers, and from these observations she gathered strength for her increasingly somber thoughts. As the years passed, she regularly assessed the situation whenever a Soviet leader died or found a new perch at the May Day parade, and although no one could remember what she'd ever said, no one could remember her ever being without something to say.

Hank Morriday, if he was honest with himself, did not even like Suzanne Smule, an antipathy built on an accumulation of slights; she managed always to look away when they passed in the corridor. She had short-clipped dark hair, thick ankles, and broad buttocks, which gave the impression of enormous hidden strength. But Hank had heard that Suzanne Smule was advising Michael Dukakis, who looked to Hank more and more like the winning horse, although others were not to be written off, especially Governor Cuomo. In any case Hank was surprised when Suzanne Smule knocked on his office door and asked, with what seemed to be genuine interest, how he was. She took the chair that faced his scratched desk and smiled earnestly. She crossed her legs, which looked a little bristly in their white stockings, and restarted her smile. Her lipstick had not been perfectly applied, so the expression became a string of pink interruptions.

"I saw you on television the other day," she said, raising her dark eyebrows. "You looked pretty good—someone who knew what he was talking about."

Hank managed a shy laugh and stroked his beard; the public television station had repeated a program that included a few of his comments on the flaws of the European social democrats and the shortage of work incentives.

"Now I know two people who saw me," he said.

"Oh, listen to Mr. Modest!" Suzanne Smule said, and crossed her legs the other way. Hank guessed she was about his age, perhaps in her late thirties, but she was far more assured. "Hey, it's good to meet you, Hank Morriday. I've kept meaning to say hello."

She smiled a wonderful smile, and Hank understood her charm at once. She wore a dark green suit loose enough to hide her stocky body. She was also wearing a perfume he'd never smelled before, a mixture of lilac and olive oil, and he noticed a long scar along the base of her neck. Hank felt wildly attracted to her, but he understood that he felt wildly attracted to virtually every female he saw— especially the ones who smiled at him. He thought about Judith Grust and his poor "performance"—a word he hated—and as Suzanne Smule talked on, Hank understood that she was flattering him, that she was trying to get him to like her, and that undoubtedly she wanted something from him.

"I'm really impressed by your thinking," she was saying, her head thrust forward, her eyes wide with sincerity.

"I think you're terrific too, Suzanne," Hank said. "And you met Gorbachev!"

Because Mikhail Gorbachev was in Washington that December week, it had been a time of unbearable excitement. At parties, in offices, at restaurants, the city was divided between those who had gotten a glimpse of the radiant Russian and those who had not; and those who had seen him were incapable of talking about anything else. Suzanne Smule was among the lucky ones, for she'd not only seen Gorbachev but had shaken his hand. "He is electric," she told Hank. "You feel the power emanating." She looked solemn and licked her imperfectly painted lips.

"Do you think," Hank asked, "that he's the real thing, or is there some kind of trick?"

"First of all, he's a Russian," Suzanne Smule replied, looking intently at Hank. "Secondly, he's the general secretary of the party. But I think that he may be a genuine reformer."

Hank felt privileged at having this private glimpse of her thoughts, but he was still baffled at this attention from a woman who'd always acted as if he did not quite exist. Her behavior made him think that something good was about to happen in his career (something Suzanne Smule already knew?), something that was drawing her to him like an ambitious moth.

Outside his office Hank could hear the clicks of keyboards, and he tried to listen when the very gaunt former deputy secretary of state, who had just returned from a hospital stay, told a joke to the former budget analyst across the hall. Hank's thoughts were a jumble; he had to get out of there.

"Let me get right to it," Suzanne Smule said. She leaned toward him, her odd perfume overpowering the air.

"I've got to ask you more about Gorbachev," Hank said, not willing to let this moment recede.

"A truly interesting leader," she said, a little impatiently. "But we'll have to see if he's another Khrushchev, or something more."

She raised her chair under her and moved it, and herself, a few inches closer.

"I came by here to get to know you better," she went on, "but I also have a favor to ask."

Suzanne Smule crossed her thick legs yet again, almost grunting as she did so. She told Hank that a friend—someone she'd known in the White House—was now at Big Tooth. Hank had heard of that? Who hadn't! Her friend wanted what she called a "sympathetic ear" and she wanted that ear connected to someone who could help her.

"The poor dear is trying to help a guy, an ex-congressman type,

who had his name smeared all over some local news program,"
Suzanne Smule said, lowering her voice. "So I thought of you—
someone who knows people who do local news. I don't know anyone local. I only do the networks; otherwise I'd have no time for
anything."

Hank's mouth twitched, but not so that anyone would notice. Did
Suzanne suspect him? She seemed to know about a lot of things,
perhaps more than she let on. He hadn't actually seen the broadcast
that mentioned Charlie Dingleman, but Judith Grust had; when she
thanked him, he had felt an odd inner trembling, as if he had sinned.
But if Suzanne was on to him, why didn't she say so? He tried to
concentrate on what she was saying as she leaned toward his desk,
her scent trailing; and he sniffed.

"Is something wrong?" she asked.

"No, of course not."

Hank was thinking that if Suzanne Smule wanted to ask for a favor, she might be ready to bestow one—especially when she scattered hints about 1988. What did Hank think? she asked. How well
did he know Mike? Hank, who had once shaken hands with the
Massachusetts governor at a reception, told Suzanne Smule that he
knew him only casually.

"I'm not sure the governor would remember," Hank said.

"Most of the people at the Institute are so dull," Suzanne Smule
said, lowering her voice. "Of course Randy Maintree is a sweetheart, but why haven't we talked before? You seem to know just how
this town operates."

Hank smiled gratefully. He watched her shift again in the chair
and noticed a dime-sized pinkness at the knee of one stocking.

"Mike is going to need a lot of help on the domestic issues," she
said, and with a soft nod she added, "He likes smart people."

As Suzanne Smule stood up to leave, she put out a hand and
grasped Hank's firmly, rewarding him with a last gust of perfume.

Then, almost as if she'd forgotten why she'd stopped by, she urged him to call her friend at Big Tooth. Candy Romulade was her name.

"You two would like each other," Suzanne Smule said. "I know you would."

"It's such a small world," he said.

"Even if you can't help her," she went on, as if she hadn't heard him, "I'd consider it a great favor if you would call. Then Candy would know that *I* was trying to help her. And that's what it's all about, isn't it?" Hank recalled those exact words from a teenage dance, the Hokey-Pokey: that's what it's all about.

FIFTEEN

JUDITH GRUST saw right through Hank Morriday. But even if he faked his empathy—his expression looking troubled, his brow slightly creased—she still liked to tell him about her quotidian annoyances, the leers of strangers such as her building superintendent, Buddy, who helped to unplug a drain and kept staring until she realized she'd left a button open. "I've never figured out why men care so much about these things," she said, pointing toward her modest possessions.

Nor could Judith figure out why something about her seemed to bother people. She knew that she was a serious person but capable of giddy laughter, and that a funny, carefree spirit lay just beneath her outward formality. Yet whenever she spoke, people seemed apprehensive, as if she were about to reveal hideous news. She couldn't be sure, but there was even something about her laugh that seemed to frighten people, especially men.

The closest that Judith had come to a serious relationship was seven years ago, with a federal prosecutor named Boyd who had started their third date by pleading his case for most of the evening, arguing (she realized later) as he might have argued before a jury, explaining that for her it was nothing—the brief internal visit of several inches of his flesh—while for him it would be a joy. He would not only be grateful for the moment but would remember it always, because with her he felt a rare sympathy.

If Judith had been deposed, she would have sworn that she liked men even if she mistrusted them and found many of them disagreeable. She would hope not to be asked about Boyd, whose internal visit had lasted for about twenty minutes (he was humming "Sixty-Minute Man," a song she could never forget) and made her sore for a week. His repeated entrances and exits in the following weeks, with her unwelcoming flesh exposed in different directions, were unpleasant, but when she insisted on a rest, he was sympathetic. She became quite fond of Boyd and imagined herself getting prosecutorial experience alongside him. Yet when Boyd was offered a job in the U.S. Attorney's office in New York, Judith found him strangely silent; he never once suggested that she join him there. That, she guessed, told her something.

She now and then thought about Miles, who was also *Law Review*, and Gary, who was in her tort class, and how she'd made both of them plead their cases. (Miles she rejected at the last minute, indifferent to his pain and suffering; to Gary she surrendered, sorrowfully, for his summation was eloquent, but he was rough when he'd promised to be gentle and did not telephone again.) She barely recalled Craig, the nearly hairless man she'd met at the Y in Washington, who always went shirtless when they were alone, but she could easily summon up the partner in Philadelphia, where she'd interned after her junior year, a man who'd crossed the line, as she put it, and then wept when she'd threatened to report him. Yet he was someone, it turned out, who seemed truly to like her and who knew people and was able to help her get hired by Thingeld, Pine & Sconce.

Judith's exercise machines had made her body taut, and her work at the firm made the rings under her eyes wider and darker. All this, she knew, bespoke the intensity of her days, yet she could not imagine living in another way. After seven years at Thingeld, Pine, she was destined for partnership; she had eighteen months to go, and although the work sometimes bored her, she was proud of its quality, particularly when it came to tax law. In hours billed she was already among the top fifteen percent; those nights and weekends had their reward, even if all the time she spent blurred into a vague collection of paper, most of which argued ridiculous questions in barely literate English and most of which succeeded only in making life for someone else more difficult and expensive.

Now and then Judith would think a little guiltily of what had happened to Charlie Dingleman, or what he had done to himself. In memory Dingleman was leering at a woman at the next table, licking his lips at the sight of those melon-shaped breasts and winking at other men in the room, where a corps of male waiters made little jokes as they served up underdone beef. Had Dingleman also touched her under the table, as her law professor had done? Judith didn't think so, but she could not forget, not ever, that the former congressman had leaned into her face and said unforgivable things in a way that suggested he was capable of hurting women. During one semester in Cambridge Judith had spent three nights as a volunteer for a rape crisis center, and *oh!* those stories left her breathless with fury. She wasn't positive that Dingleman was like those men, but he might have been. And it all made sense when Pete Thingeld told her that Dingleman had a sexual disorder, one so horrible that Judith could only begin to imagine it.

If Judith had been told that she had actually wrecked Charlie Dingleman's life, she would have conceded that the punishment was out of proportion to her ruined lunch. But life was full of dilemmas and this one had become like a catchy and repulsive tune, much like "Sixty-Minute Man," capturing her senses. Whenever Judith felt ashamed, she would review the argument she'd fashioned for herself: she had done Dingleman—and the country—a favor; she had helped to teach him a lesson in the nick of time, while he could still get expert help. She did want to be fair, to do what was best, and if she was wrong, well, she regretted that, but it was Hank Morriday's fault too.

Judith sometimes woke up with a sense that she was drifting on a raft to which she could not quite cling. If she regarded other associates with contempt, particularly the ones who would never make partner, she envied the flippant ones who had decided, sometimes with a laugh, to leave the firm and even the profession. It took real commitment to stay on the partnership track, and even so things could go awry. They could ask you to stay for another year, and then they could ask you to leave. Judith had seen it happen.

Whenever her mother called from Pittsburgh, Judith always said that everything was fine. She could not bear to get into one of their discussions about what her mother called "the world as it is" or to hear how important it was "simply to relax." Judith's mother had gone to law school herself, but that had been another generation; she had married a stockbroker and decided it was more satisfying to spend her days playing tennis and raising a child. She had become a very good tennis player.

When she asked Judith in a girlish whisper if she had a boyfriend, Judith would describe someone who resembled Hank Morriday but wasn't quite Hank. The Hank described by Judith had been a personal friend of Jimmy Carter's and had all sorts of ties to important Democrats. This Hank was also writing a book on welfare policy that was bound to be very influential.

As she heard herself saying such things, Judith would wish that she was fonder of the real Hank Morriday or that he was more like her imaginary Hank. At least when they'd tried it again, he didn't leave her sore, although his beard scratched. But he didn't care about the law or who'd make partner this year, and she had to admit that she didn't care about the book he'd been writing for too long. In that way Hank was beginning to be a terrific bore, and even worse, he did not even seem very interested in his own work. The last time they'd gone out, he'd talked about finding a job with what he kept calling the Dukakis administration, as if he knew someone close to Mike, as he kept calling him. Worst of all Hank could do nothing—nothing at all—to help her at Thingeld, Pine & Sconce.

Someone who could help her was Alfred Schmalz, who for several months had been exceedingly friendly. Alfred Schmalz was the saddest man she'd ever known, and sometimes Judith would see him at his desk, his watery blue eyes staring into a world all his own, his thin gray hair slick on top and a little long around the ears, his tongue licking his lower, discolored lip.

Judith knew that Alfred Schmalz had once done something big in the State Department and that he always wore dark suits and barely moved his head, even when he nodded in greeting, and that he had been with the firm forever. They'd really talked for the first time on a Saturday morning last summer, when they'd both brought their mugs to the coffeepot and he'd smiled sadly at the woman, more than thirty years younger, in her crimson sweatshirt and freshly ironed jeans. Even on a Saturday in August Alfred Schmalz wore a coat and tie, although his summer coat was linen (and would turn to brown tweed as winter came in).

"I know this will seem an odd thing to say, but you remind me of my late wife," he told Judith in a soft voice, and looked tenderly at her. "Not so much any one thing, but the way you appear as a whole person."

"I've always admired your work," Judith replied, and she mentioned a generic drug case that for every law student had made his name eponymous.

"I know you've been one of our most valuable associates," he said, licking his discolored lip. "I've heard many good things about you; you're very highly thought of here." He stared at her, his eyes now fixed upon Judith's. "Forgive me, Miss Grust. That resemblance I mentioned to you—it seemed to upset you."

"Oh no, certainly not," she said, although that wasn't quite true. Schmalz looked at that moment so awkward that Judith felt awkward too and turned to fill her coffee mug, a white one with her name reduced to a childish "Judi." When she turned, Schmalz was gone.

. . .

A FEW WEEKS LATER, in the early fall, Schmalz had invited Judith to lunch in the partners' oval dining room, a bright place with paintings by unknown Washington colorists and the best view of K Street. He was working at the time on a bank merger and wanted Judith's advice. But during lunch (a cold soup, followed by broiled grouper) he spoke about his family, his grown children and his one grandchild, a nine-year-old who was so argumentative that (Schmalz chuckled) he was bound to become a lawyer. Melancholy filled the room like cold steam as the serving woman brought food, poured coffee, and cleared away crumbs.

Weeks passed, and sometimes Alfred Schmalz would linger at Judith's office door to talk about the weather or the Redskins or events. When Gorbachev came to town, Schmalz told Judith excitedly that he'd seen the Russian outside the Soviet embassy and had never felt so hopeful about the future; he could imagine his grandson on a playground with little Russian children, jumping rope in a peaceful world. As Christmas approached, Judith found it natural to stop by Schmalz's office and chat for a moment, asking perhaps about his disputatious grandson or some point of law. It was also during the holiday season of late 1987 (for her mother Judith had bought a seventy-five-dollar book with photographs of tennis stars) that a woman named Candy Romulade telephoned. Judith almost didn't take the call—she didn't know the name—but she'd certainly heard of Big Tooth.

"I believe," Candy Romulade said a little tentatively, "that you know my client, Congressman Dingleman."

"What is it you're actually trying to say?" Judith replied, a favorite phrase. She felt her throat tighten.

"Is this a bad time?" Candy Romulade asked.

Judith heard a shard of doubt enter her caller's voice.

"It sounds like it's a bad time for you," Judith said, parrying. "You're not making yourself clear," she added, thrusting.

"I think you know what I'm talking about," the woman from Big Tooth said, still hesitant.

"I have no idea," Judith said.

"I think you do," the woman went on, sounding no more confident, "and I wonder if you're even aware of the damage you've done."

Judith breathed a little shallowly. It was strange to hear that she really had hurt Dingleman; and although she did, in a distant way, pity him, she could not deny feeling a kind of satisfaction.

"He's a very obnoxious man," Judith said, choosing each word with care. "But I still don't have any idea what you're talking about." Who could trace it back to her?

"I think I'll need to talk to you again," the woman from Big Tooth said.

"I can't imagine why," Judith replied, as her eyes blinked rapidly. "If you're threatening me," she went on, sounding certain of herself, "I advise you to be very careful."

. . .

ALFRED SCHMALZ surprised Judith when he invited her to a holiday dinner, a very special occasion, the annual gathering of Schmalzes on the first Saturday after New Year's Day. When he put his head into her office, he looked smaller and paler than he had just a few days before.

"You must come. My children will be there, and my grandson,

the one I've told you about. And perhaps some other friends who need a bit of post-holiday cheer."

"I'd love to," Judith replied at once, and watched Alfred Schmalz put on a rare, sad smile and lick his purplish lower lip.

Judith knew that wasn't nice of her. Without looking at her calendar, she knew that she had another engagement: she had promised to accompany Hank Morriday to the Institute's annual black-tie dinner, an event that meant a lot to him, and even more so because the speaker this year was Governor Dukakis. But Judith felt sure that Hank would understand her change of plans when she explained how lonely Alfred Schmalz was, how pathetic really. Hank though did not seem to understand. "It's because he's a big partner; I'm not dumb," he said.

"Well, it's true, Hank, that it is very difficult for a lowly associate like me to turn down an invitation from a big partner like him," Judith said, adding, "I don't see why you have to give me a hard time about it."

Then before Judith could accuse him of accusing her of something more, Hank hung up with a smack. She shrugged, wondering how anyone could get so upset over a boring banquet with people in formal dress and a speaker who seemed to be on television all the time, saying the same thing. But she didn't want Hank to be annoyed with her, especially not when she thought about that pushy woman, Candy Romulade.

SIXTEEN

SOMETIMES WHEN she left her office, Teresa Maracopulos wondered how her life would be if, instead of going home, she ran away. She would imagine starting over, perhaps with someone really interesting, like Reynolds Mund, at the same time realizing that she could never do it. Martin belonged to her like an unsought relative, and she bore some responsibility for his happiness.

But Martin was looking at her suspiciously, and it didn't help that a few days earlier, when he'd called Big Tooth, Candy Romulade had told him that Teresa had been away from her desk since lunch. When Martin asked if she knew where she was, Candy hesitated and said, "I'm sure I can't say," which wasn't true: Candy could have said that Teresa was at the television station and that she was spending too much time there. That night when Teresa got into bed and sensed Martin's hand approaching, she shook herself, as if to brush off a mosquito. Martin persisted, though, making Teresa ticklish, and she twitched. "For some reason it feels uncomfortable tonight," she said.

Martin let loose a hiss, which surprised Teresa. "What's going on?" he asked, a question so broad that Teresa formulated several potential guilty replies before shaking her head.

"What do you mean?"

"I mean with this," he said, and she felt his hand between her legs.

"If you want to, Martin, I guess we can," she said, and stroked his cheek.

Martin shook his head and sat up. "What's going on?" he asked again, the question becoming larger in the quiet of their bedroom. When she said nothing, Martin let her know that her life was not as secret as she'd thought. "When I call your office, you're gone," he said. "Your car has hundreds of miles more than it should on it—"

"You're checking *up* on me?" Teresa interrupted him. "You're looking at the mileage of the car?"

Martin looked offended. "I'm the one who gets the oil changed around here," he said, "so I look. But you've been acting different," he continued. "There's a guy in our office, his wife just left him, and the way he'd talk about her, she sounded just like you."

Teresa's heart beat faster. "We don't have a great marriage," she heard herself saying. "You don't seem to respect what I do."

Martin said nothing. He was staring at her angrily.

"You don't respect what *I* do, is what it is," he said.

"Maybe we need to get away from each other," she replied. "Just for a while."

Martin looked shocked. "You want 'more space' or something?" he said, with all the sarcasm he could muster.

"I'm very confused," she replied, a little surprised at her own words. "I guess I didn't mean what I said."

One of them must have accidentally pressed the remote, for their television lit up, and there was the weatherman, his pointer jabbing a snow-covered New England, and there was the coanchor with the long, streaked hair, and soon enough, the anchorman took over again. Teresa found herself paying more attention to his flickering face than to her husband, who was saying something accusatory just as Reynolds Mund said something she couldn't quite understand, something about a fuse in the schools, she thought at first. When Martin shook her, the first time he had ever done that—"You're not even *listening* to me!" he said—her mouth quivered and she felt almost glad to have the excuse to run from their house, as if to catch up with the television picture. But after she got dressed and actually stepped outside, the dark and silent street felt dangerous. She returned to Martin, who had stood in the doorway and begged her not to go and then asked for forgiveness. "I love you so much," he said, and she embraced him because she knew that was true.

. . .

AT BIG TOOTH work surrounded everyone with confidential goings-on, and Teresa had her own secrets. She usually told Candy Romulade everything, but not about Reynolds Mund, the way he whispered that peculiar stuff about "news molecules," and how she liked visiting the television station and was hoping to learn about the news business. Reynolds had told her that she had a good voice.

But if Teresa kept her secrets, others at Big Tooth had begun to pay more attention to her. For the first time she was ordered to the office of a partner, the former secretary of commerce, a sandy-haired man named Dennis who wore buttoned-down shirts and bright ties, which he hoped would make him look younger than his sixty-two years. Dennis lisped scornfully when he discovered tasks that Teresa had left undone, such as forgetting to make appointments on Capitol Hill for an aerospace company whose new missile could be programmed to scream *"Up yours, buster!"* as it struck a target. But Teresa had heard that Dennis too was under pressure; an important client, a psychotic Latin American colonel who'd wanted to open an orphanage, had moved his account to a Big Tooth competitor.

"You've been here for a long time; you ought to know better," Dennis said, and at that he tapped one of the Christmas cards lining his desk, knocking over a row of them. "Is it the season? Whatever it is, you can't just go disappearing for hours at a time when people need you."

Teresa shook her head, abject. "I'm sorry," she said.

Dennis liked people to call him Mr. Secretary. Teresa remembered that and by her third Mr. Secretary he seemed less severe. His thin hair always looked too curly, almost permed, and he had a habit of pursing his lips. But although she feared the worst, he spoke to her not unkindly.

"Your behavior is erratic," he said. "We worry that you might do something to compromise the firm."

Then he stood and turned his back to her.

"Is it something about my work?" Teresa asked in a squeaky voice.

"I don't think I could be much clearer, Teresa," he said, looking down from his window, not seeing her persistent smile. "You should be doing more to help Candy."

"I am helping," she said. When he said nothing to that, she added, "I like working for you, Mr. Secretary, because you're so understanding," and when he still didn't turn from the window, she realized that Dennis was one of those rare men who were not attracted to her.

Dennis smiled and patted his hair with two fingers. When she murmured what sounded like "Thank you," he said something about hoping she'd be able to stay at Big Tooth in spite of everything. Teresa was happy to escape his office, but there was no escaping the mistrustful thoughts that pursued her.

. . .

CANDY ROMULADE meanwhile was experiencing holiday sadness, and one day she told Teresa about her grandmother, who had danced around the Yule tree as a child in her native Switzerland and had hoped to pass on this dance to her American descendants. But so far, apart from Candy, there were no American descendants. Candy's mood wasn't helped by Charlie Dingleman, who was beginning to sound as if he'd lost confidence in her. She worried that she'd made a mistake in calling Judith Grust, but as she told Charlie repeatedly, it took time to rebuild a reputation. She knew that she was getting short-tempered and was sorry when she snapped at Teresa. She also knew that she was smoking too much; Teresa complained that it was getting hard to breathe around there.

On a dark late-December day Candy looked down from their window onto K Street, and Teresa got up and stood beside her. A ragged assortment of Santas stood on two corners, ringing bells for the Salvation Army, but not much money was coming their way. At times Washington seemed not so much a city as a bunch of stage sets where strangers acted out their brief, curious parts. As they watched the crowds with their dazzling shopping bags, Candy suddenly hugged Teresa, and simultaneously a single tear trickled down Teresa's left cheek as one started from Candy's right eye.

"I don't know what to do," Teresa suddenly told her office friend. "Martin thinks that something is wrong. They think something is wrong with me here. Maybe they're right."

"I don't know either," Candy said, and confessed that she was mortally afraid that Charlie Dingleman would take his account elsewhere. That would finish her at Big Tooth, it really would. "I want people to trust me," Candy said sorrowfully, smoking two cigarettes in quick succession. "I'm also starting to hate my job," she added, and then tried without success to take back her rash words.

SEVENTEEN

ONE FEBRUARY NIGHT Charlie Dingleman thought that he was vanishing. He went to a book party for a retired diplomat and waited in line to get his own copy of *My Four Trouble Spots* signed by the memoirist, who had a thin face and a canny expression. Charlie recognized many of the other guests, who were nibbling cheese clumps and sipping warm white wine from plastic cups and chatting, especially about the upcoming Iowa caucuses (where Senator Dole was destined to defeat Vice President Bush). He nodded to a network correspondent, a Midwestern senator, and the old woman he'd run into a couple of months ago in Dumbarton Oaks, the journalist's widow. No one looked directly at Charlie, although the senator greeted him with a rubbery handshake before moving on, as if Charlie had been part of a long receiving line. When Charlie reached the author, the retired diplomat's smile stayed in place and he looked up with his slightly hooded eyes as he tried to remember who Charlie was. He inscribed Charlie's copy, "With best wishes, always," and the book soon found a spot beside Charlie's large bed.

The house on R Street was being depleted by Eve's raids, each one timed to Charlie's absences. It was almost as if she were watching the place; one day Charlie went out for a walk and thirty minutes later an antique chair was gone. The house itself was suffering. Water stains had bubbled across the ceiling of the main bedroom, and Charlie fretted that the leakage was new, that he'd soon have to pay for roof repairs. One morning as Charlie lay in bed contemplating his future, he pounded the mattress and swore. He swore at having lost two wives, his seat in Congress, and now perhaps his reputation, over a murmur of a rumor. For the first time he felt something like panic; he got out of bed and began to read the thin Big Tooth brochure that Candy had given him, one that promised "strategic analysis and advocacy communications at the highest level." Then he got back into bed again.

"Charlie, what's the matter?" Candy asked when he called, sounding, he knew, a little breathless.

"Nothing's happened," he replied. "The White House should be talking to me, but nothing's happened. Let's give it up, Candy."

"There could be any explanation," she said in a motherly singsong. "They could be on vacation. Don't panic!"

Charlie shook his head. He thought of her slim legs and the old skin of her face and the shiny incomprehension of her eyes. He did say, "Pols like me are realists, Candy. That's the one thing I do know."

He sensed her shaking her head. "Things were going our way," she told him. "That rumor about you is dead, dead, dead. And I haven't even gotten started. I'm about to get our story out—how a good man was defamed. I think we're close."

"But you haven't done it. I'm done for," Charlie said.

"I've prepared this whole action plan for you," she said. "It breaks my heart to hear you talk about giving up. I'm trying to arrange a one-on-one with someone."

"Don't you see?" Charlie said. "Something about me scares them."

Charlie feared that every second of this conversation would appear on his bill, yet even as he tried to end it, her words—this talk about a "one-on-one"—gave him hope. She said again, a little desperately he thought, that all was not yet lost, and it was only when Charlie heard footsteps that he hurried to get off the phone. Of course he recognized the footsteps.

Eve had a peculiar surprised smile when she saw Charlie on the edge of the bed. She had not yet taken off her winter coat (made of rabbit, he remembered) and her face was bright pink from the cold.

"I thought you'd be at work," she said with a sympathetic squint.

"Is there something you forgot to take—something you missed?"

"Don't be angry, Charlie," she said. "Things happen."

Eve took off her coat and carefully hung it in the closet that otherwise contained only Charlie's clothing. She sat beside him on the bed and put an arm on his shoulder. Charlie breathed her familiar perfume and observed her sharp, long nose and slender hands.

"I worry about you," she said.

Charlie looked into her eyes and tried to find a glint of sympathy.

"I do, Charlie," she said. "I worry about what's happening to you."

Charlie looked at her determined face in the winter light and saw that she still didn't know about his other difficulty. Her skin shone, and the curved tip of her long nose twitched slightly. She looked grimly back, and moved a few inches away. Charlie regarded her delicate hands, her parted lips, and wondered what she might permit, for old times' sake. They stared into each other's eyes.

"You know," he said, "I may just move back to Pennsylvania, to the old district."

Even as he said this, he could not imagine living among all those people who'd turned on him. But Eve nodded with approval at this declaration and said, "We all need a change." She leaned toward him, she squinted again, and her nose wrinkled. Then she kissed him, and the softness of her lips lingered. Charlie tried to repeat the experience.

"Not a good idea," she said, and stood up and went to the closet to fetch her coat.

"Is it like I've vanished?" Charlie asked, his self-pity burning away caution.

Eve shook her head, not quite following his thoughts. He now noticed that, in addition to her coat, she was carrying a blue-and-red Ferragamo tie that she'd given him on his forty-seventh birthday. "You never liked it," she said, "and it's really mine."

Then it was hers, and she was gone for good.

. . .

SEVERAL DAYS LATER Charlie started reading *My Four Trouble Spots*, where the author in his introduction wrote, "I have hoped to set down vivid portraits of world leaders I have met, or had occasion to brush sleeves with, in the course of a long career that has taken me near and far in the service of my country." Memorably the author had "brushed sleeves" with Chiang Kai-shek, next to whom he'd stood at an embassy urinal:

> I noticed, or believed I noticed, that the austere Chinaman seemed to be glancing my way, as if to see whether his device "measured up" to the one attached to the gruff Yankee beside him.
>
> I made a small joke. "This is really the pause that refreshes," I said to Chiang, with a grin.
>
> The Chinese leader looked at me, perplexed.
>
> "This is something that surmounts boundaries and creeds," I went on. "If Mao Tse-tung were here in the next stall, who knows what might come of it?"
>
> My witticism contained a grain of seriousness, but it was only then that I realized the former warlord did not speak a word of English. I wonder what he thought I was saying! To this day, I'll never know.

The dust jacket revealed that the retired diplomat was now serving as an "adjunct adviser" to President Reagan, and it was an odd coincidence that Charlie was taking note of this when Skip Haine called.

"I've been trying your office today," Skip said, lying smoothly. "Someone is not taking messages there."

"How are you, Skip?" Charlie asked.

"I'm fine, sir. But I'm afraid I've got some not very good news for you."

"I can imagine," Charlie said, and even though this call was no real surprise, his heart began to beat with unpleasant speed.

"That little bump we were passing turned into a pothole," Skip Haine said. "A big pothole."

"I had that feeling, Skip," Charlie said, keeping his voice casual.

"The FBI report came in and it makes us a little jittery, sir, although we don't believe a single allegation."

"Give me an allegation," Charlie said.

"That's confidential, sir."

"Yeah, but give me a clue, Skip," Charlie said, his teeth grinding, his thoughts congealing.

"You know we can't compromise sources, sir, but let me put it this way: if it's true, I'm sure you know what it is, and if it's not true, there's nothing for you to worry about."

"And this means . . . ?"

"We're putting your appointment on indefinite hold."

Charlie nodded, as if Skip Haine were in the room.

"You've got to understand that this has nothing to do with you," Skip went on, trying to be cheerful. "But the president is in a very delicate situation now, what with the business about—you know, Iran and all that—and frankly, Congressman, he doesn't see you helping."

Charlie shook his head.

"Are you there?" said Skip Haine.

"Where else?"

"The hope over at our shop," Skip continued, "is that the vice president wins in November. Your friends can put in a good word for you then, and let me tell you, you have a lot of friends. But that's the best I can say, Congressman, at this point."

Charlie said that he understood, but even as the call ended, he did not understand. He wondered if he should call back and ask for a lesser job, at a lower rank—perhaps deputy assistant to the president or even special assistant—duties that were less sensitive. The title, which he had once regarded with almost military respect, didn't matter. Like a vision Charlie saw the face of Alfred Schmalz, filled with sadness, and Anthony "Pete" Thingeld, his wall covered with pictures of himself, and he felt the deathly boredom overtake him and squeeze his heart. He could not stand this, he told himself. Maybe he really should return to Pennsylvania and hang out his shingle; he thought about fresh air and parking space. Or he might write his own memoirs, just like that former ambassador; he'd brushed at least as many sleeves. He picked up the telephone and, before he could think more about it, dialed the 703 number that led to the house in McLean where his ex-wife Abigail lived. She didn't answer, and when he heard her machine, he didn't leave a message. Perhaps, he thought, she was out with James, and he found that he was a little alarmed by the solidity, the permanence, of that name.

EIGHTEEN

Hank Morriday leaned forward slightly, as if trying to hear what the angry Iranian cab driver was saying, although he was paying not the slightest attention. A large vein throbbed in the center of the driver's shiny head, and as they raced down Fourteenth Street, past the prostitutes in short, bright skirts, Hank kept repeating, "I know what you mean." Flapping against the windshield, attached by a blue string to the rearview mirror, was a penciled, ecumenical prayer wrapped in plastic that said, "Jesus, see me in most evil of worlds, and show me the way to Allah." Hank mouthed the prayer to himself as the driver made a looping right turn from the left lane in order to speed down the ugly remnants of K Street, braking suddenly when the traffic thickened. "Damn fucking cherry blossoms," the cab driver said—the curse of spring. It took several more minutes before he was able to drop Hank in front of the yellow brick building that jutted out over the sidewalk.

It was late March, a little after six o'clock, and there was still faded light over the flat city. As Hank stepped from the cab (which began pulling away even as he closed the door, the driver mumbling fresh oaths), he bit his lip and rubbed his thumb in uncertain anticipation of a first date, trying to remember all that he had heard about Candy Romulade. He saw his reflection in a window and wished that he'd worn something else; his pants looked wrinkled and his blazer felt one size too small. He tugged at his belt, which had gained a notch, and stroked his beard in quest of hairy symmetry. He was jittery and thought about the dangling prayer as he went through the revolving door into the onrushing darkness of the lobby.

It had been nearly three months since Judith Grust had canceled their evening at the Institute's annual gala, but Hank was still annoyed about that. He could barely remember the dinner, although Dukakis had given a speech about good jobs and good wages and Suzanne Smule had arrived with one of Dukakis's lieutenants at her side, and had smiled at him. In any case, snit or no snit, Judith seemed to have lost interest, which surprised Hank, considering how intimate they'd been on (he counted) two and one-half occasions. The void of his social life had made it easier to telephone Candy Romulade, whom Suzanne Smule had described as "bright and pretty and blond, but she needs a man."

The first time they'd talked, in early January, Hank did as he'd been instructed and mumbled something about helping out a client—"some congressman." Candy Romulade immediately asked Hank for names and Hank mentioned a couple of journalists—people that Candy knew too. In late January Hank called again, just to see how things were going, he said. When he telephoned a month later, Candy said that the congressman was no longer a client, but why not get together anyway? They then scheduled and postponed several evenings, and each time they spoke, Hank thought that Candy sounded tense. Sometimes she talked so rapidly that he couldn't understand a word. Still, Suzanne Smule had said that she was pretty and blond, so Hank was hopeful when the elevator reached Big Tooth's floor. His female companionship in recent weeks had been entirely imaginary, unless one reckoned with Wendy Lullabay, the much-photographed actress in *Perfect Fit*, who regularly surrendered to Hank's needs, so to speak.

As Hank stepped from the elevator he found himself facing the receptionist, whose dark lips were in a pout, her inflated hair defying gravity. Behind her, with a drooping cherry blossom tacked above it, was the Big Tooth logo, two front teeth sunk into the planet. When Hank said that he was there to see Candy Romulade, the receptionist yawned and said, "If you'll just have a seat," managing not to look at Hank.

In the bright light his shoes looked scuffed and he noticed a tiny stain high up on his trousers. He remained standing and then paced, which seemed to distract the receptionist: her eyes followed him. Hank glanced at the wall and the framed photographs of Big Tooth's founders—the senator, the astronaut, the commerce secretary, the presidential counselor—and when he heard a door open, he turned with a smile, expecting Candy. Instead he saw a man with a very bushy mustache and a military uniform that included huge epaulets; Hank nodded, but something about the man's black eyes terrified him, and he looked away as the receptionist said, "Good night, General." On a low table, next to the morning newspaper and several magazines, Hank saw a stiff, cream-colored card covered with gold-and-black script announcing an event that evening— something to raise money for a hopeless social cause. When he looked up and saw a thin woman with dark blond hair and a wrinkled tan, he barely paid attention, until she began to speak to him and to apologize for keeping him waiting.

"You're Candy Romulade," he said, when he deduced this.

"I just have to make one more phone call, then I'll be right out, sorry," she said, speaking even more rapidly than she had on the phone. He saw lines of tension streaking about her face when she attempted a smile. Before she gave a little wave and turned, she stared brightly at him, and Hank tried to see if disappointment was trapped in her gaze as it must have been in his own. He observed her slim legs and thought about the apprehension in her eyes.

"She's so uptight," the receptionist said when Candy had gone, still not looking at Hank. She shook her hair, as if for emphasis.

As the receptionist looked at her wristwatch, Hank thought about the Institute, where people had been absorbed by the presidential primaries. Now they referred to Michael Dukakis as if he were a favored uncle; even those who'd once sworn total allegiance to Babbitt or Gephardt or Jackson or Gore boasted of their ties to the governor. Suzanne Smule still dropped hints that there might be a place for Hank in this Dukakis set, but it was getting late and he often had the feeling that he was being judged and that the judgments were not favorable. He sensed a special hostility from a recently appointed Fellow named Crane, who was supposed to be close to Dukakis and was working on a study about welfare that sounded much like Hank's. To Hank's horror people sometimes confused the two of them, because Crane, like Hank, had thick eyebrows, receding dark hair, and a beard that needed a trim. Hank was thinking about Crane, his doppelganger, when the Big Tooth receptionist stood up and fetched a rose-colored coat from a closet.

"That's a good color for you," Hank said.

She seemed not to hear.

"Good color," he said again, venturing a smile that was not a success.

"Thanks," she said, and was gone, her lips pressed together.

Hank felt a tap on his shoulder and turned to see a sandy-haired man with an inquiring expression. "You're taken care of?" the man asked. "I'm Dennis, one of the partners."

Hank nodded, and nodded again as two more Big Tooth employees made their way out, both of them about Hank's age, both dressed in suits that were far more expensive than anything he could afford. It had been more than ten minutes since Candy Romulade's first, rushed appearance.

"I *am* sorry," Candy said when she reappeared, and this time she dropped her arms in an expression of friendly weariness.

Hank tried to mimic this expression but already had a feeling that things were not going well. And yet . . . did she not look more attractive than she had minutes before? There was more color in her face, and as she drew closer and offered him a thin arm, he inhaled a perfume that he recognized as the scent used by Suzanne Smule.

"I had to take a call," she said, not quite meeting Hank's eyes, "because I may be getting a very hot new client."

Hank supposed he ought to ask who that was, but he did not really care, and then it slipped his mind as a short, slightly plump, pretty woman appeared. That was Teresa Maracopulos, whose mind seemed to be entirely elsewhere as the three of them rode the elevator and then stepped onto K Street, where Teresa waved and trotted off to her parking garage.

"You didn't ask me who my new client was," Candy said, almost accusingly.

"Of course I want to know," Hank replied, watching as she reached into her purse and lit a cigarette. "Was it that guy I saw leaving, in the uniform?"

Candy chuckled and then smiled as if Hank were a little dim-witted.

"Of course not," she said. "The partners handle all the international clients." Candy seemed surprised that Hank hadn't recognized the general, for people said that he had killed hundreds of disloyal peasants before the coup and quite a few nuns too. "I'm doing Reynolds Mund," Candy went on. "I'm going to plan his twentieth anniversary gala; it just got set in stone." She seemed unusually happy as she tossed her barely smoked cigarette onto the pavement. She lit another cigarette and said, "I'm going to drag you to a party tonight. You don't have to go if you don't want to."

"I'm game," Hank assured her, remembering the cream-colored invitation.

"We don't have to stay long," she said, biting down on a lip. She immediately flung down her new cigarette. "I quit these for two years," she said.

Candy said something else to herself as he followed her halfway into the street, where among the rows of traffic she reached for a taxicab with one fender missing. When Hank climbed after her into the backseat (Candy was already giving a Georgetown address), he felt her right shoulder pressing against him and wondered (compared with other recent pressings) if that meant something. In the dimness of the veering car, as he stared at her shadowed profile, she looked just as pretty as he had imagined.

. . .

WHEN THEY ARRIVED in front of a four-story brick house on N Street, Candy was saying, "There'll be some Dukakis people there, but I can't promise you it will be much fun."

The front door opened and a brightly dressed crowd surrounded them. The rooms were small and densely furnished with antique tables and unread books. Ethiopian waiters in white coats carried hors d'oeuvres and a pretty woman wearing a bow tie brought trays of wine and seltzer. Hank's heart stopped, for he had been at this very party many times and he had never gotten used to it.

Across the room he saw the Austrian diplomat who had refused to go back to Vienna when his tour was up; close to him, holding a pale yellow drink, was the former United States senator who called himself Former Senator when he telephoned strangers; there, laughing out loud, was a newspaper columnist, Brandon Sladder, who often appeared on television and spoke with such authority that he was in wide demand; nearby was an automobile dealer who had occasionally been indicted for fraud but provided bargains to his circle of friends. Hank recognized others: a Jesuit who was known to drink too much and talk with regret about the women he'd turned down, two women named Muffy, an elegant couple with waxy skin. And the crowd kept growing.

Because Hank had been in Washington for so many years, he also found himself greeting people he almost knew. When he saw Suzanne Smule wearing a pink dress that revealed a cluster of tiny blemishes at the base of her neck, she seemed at first not to recognize him; when he insisted on moving closer, she offered him a cold cheek, upon which he placed his lips, and looked triumphant when she spotted Candy Romulade.

"So you two have finally gotten together," Suzanne Smule said, and then, to Candy, with a meaningful look, "I meant to call you."

"You couldn't have reached me—an office *crise*," Candy confided. "You can't believe what's going on."

Hank offered a curious smile. "Hey, tell me," he said.

Both women ignored him. Candy Romulade, standing close to Suzanne Smule, looked thinner and more worn out; she looked like someone perpetually eager to be done with whatever she was doing.

"There are some people you should meet," Suzanne Smule said, looking more at Candy than at Hank. "You must definitely say hello."

With those words she stretched a chubby arm and produced, as if magically, a bald man with rimless glasses and a reddish blond mustache.

"This is Gordon," Suzanne Smule said, saying his last name so softly that Hank could not hear it. "Gordon is very, very key to Mike's operation. Everybody wants to hire him."

Gordon smiled into his mustache.

"You're too kind," he said.

"Hank is with me, at the Institute," Suzanne Smule said. "He's good," she assured Gordon.

Gordon did not seem persuaded, and when his eyes met Hank's there was no sign of interest in anything that Hank might have to say.

"The governor really appreciated your thoughts on Gorbachev,"

Gordon said to Suzanne Smule, then beamed genuinely when he saw a pretty woman with shiny dark hair and large brown eyes whose name, Hank thought, was Robin. Gordon went at once to Robin's side.

Hank's face turned red, and he looked at Candy Romulade, who did not seem to notice that Gordon had gone away. Suzanne Smule was smiling at someone else as a waiter came by and offered a tray of asparagus spears wrapped in bacon. Hank took one and felt something like butter heading toward his wrist.

"I want you to meet one of the governor's domestic people," Suzanne Smule was saying, pointing to someone who looked very much like Hank, although a decade younger. He had Hank's dark, curly hair and black beard and (Hank saw, as if in a mirror) his slight potbelly. "I can't believe you haven't found each other already," she added. "After all, you're both at the Institute."

Candy Romulade had an expectant look, but Hank did not, for the object of Suzanne Smule's enthusiasm was of course Hank's doppelganger, Crane. A moment later, en route to Crane, Hank was stopped by the chubby Austrian diplomat, whose name was Joachim, and by his wife.

"*Ach*, we meet again, my good fellow!" the Austrian said, showing off a green incisor when he smiled. "It is so fantastic, this city, this endless round of entertaining; there is no place like it, not even our Vienna."

His wife extended a moist, small hand to Hank.

"My name," she said, "is Gretel." She lowered her voice and whispered: "I have heard that Governor Dukakis himself is coming this evening. Have you heard?"

Her eyes became wider. "Surely you must know," the Austrian said, at which point it became obvious to Hank that they were confusing him with Crane.

Hank shook his head, excused himself, and soon was heading toward Candy, surprised at her tight expression as she talked to Crane. She was sucking deeply on a cigarette and was the only one smoking. As Hank approached her, reaching for a toothpick jabbed through a shrimp, he saw that Suzanne Smule had fallen into conversation with a thin-faced former diplomat—the author of *My Four Trouble Spots*, which everyone in Washington had praised for its prose and its insights. It was becoming very warm inside and Hank spotted sweat on the pale, blemished skin just below Suzanne Smule's neck and smelled her perfume of lilac and olive oil.

"I've just met the most delightful man!" Suzanne Smule began telling Hank, and introduced him to the diplomat-author.

"People have been kind," he said, looking for a moment a little dazed. "I've just been lucky enough to have had memorable experiences to write about."

Then it was Suzanne Smule's turn to mysteriously vanish in the middle of a sentence, and Hank felt tugs on his sleeve. "To my surprise," the former diplomat was saying, "my book has had a modest success. It's actually been bought by people who are not necessarily my friends."

He chuckled, his pleased, cunning expression now fastened on Hank. He talked about the pleasure he'd had in writing about his life and how once he'd sat in a toilet stall next to Andrei Gromyko. "He farted like a machine gun!" he whispered confidentially. "I left that out of my book." Hank promised that he would buy a copy soon.

"You're working with Governor Dukakis," the ex-diplomat went on, leaning eagerly forward even as Hank shook his head. "He's a good man—a sensible fellow."

Hank was feeling warm, so warm in fact that he wondered if he could keep down those pieces of asparagus and bacon and shrimp, and as the diplomat-author was telling him something about a visit to Hungary, he saw someone very familiar heading across the room—so familiar that it took Hank a moment to recognize Judith Grust, who looked older in the company of the sad-faced man with the slightly discolored lower lip. They both stared, and when it became certain that they would have to greet each other, Hank walked over and bent to kiss Judith's cheek.

"Hank, it's so good to see you," she said with an earnestness that seemed to make her eyes dilate.

"Me too," he replied, and for a moment they clasped hands. "It's such a small place, our town."

Judith nodded and said, "This is my friend—my friend and colleague and, I must confess, mentor—Alfred Schmalz," and she smiled at her companion, who wore a dark suit and whose head didn't seem able to move, for he looked straight ahead and not at Hank.

As they shook hands, Hank saw Candy Romulade dashing across the room, almost aloft in her high heels, her cigarette held above her head. She approached the three of them and, ignoring Judith and Alfred Schmalz, took Hank's arm and said, "Please, please, there's someone I want you to meet." She tugged at him and, when he didn't move, pointed to the author of *My Four Trouble Spots*, saying, "I may take him on as a client. He has a book that everyone in Washington is talking about."

Hank retrieved his arm and smiled a little apologetically at Judith and Alfred Schmalz. He wanted Judith to know that he was seeing someone—and not someone thirty years older than himself, either. Who *was* that guy? He then presented Candy Romulade to Judith Grust and to Alfred Schmalz and vice versa.

"I know your name," Candy said to Judith, and lit another cigarette.

"And I know yours," Judith replied, a little uneasily. They stared at each other until both of them remembered why that was so.

NINETEEN

O<small>N A LATE</small> Thursday in March Charlie Dingleman began once more to read *My Four Trouble Spots*. He couldn't sleep because he had an appointment the next morning with Pete Thingeld and knew that nothing good was in store. He checked the index, as if his own name might magically appear, and turned to a passage in which the author bade farewell to his "second trouble spot." Charlie found that the text was becalming:

I knew that a new president would want to replace me with "his own man," no matter how well I had accomplished the delicate tasks with which I'd been charged. I knew we soon would be leaving our lovingly tended, spotlessly clean home, and that it would be particularly hard on Mara, our servant of three years, who had developed such a keen affection for my wife and me. (It was a fondness that was wholly reciprocated; we called her "Mara-Nara," in appreciation of her skill at the stove and with the broom.) I remembered what I'd once been told by my tutor at Oxford in the course of a very small dinner party: "You must find that rock-hard spot within yourself and cling to it for duty and country." So I held on to that spot and attempted to leave with dry eyes. But Mara—our dear Mara-Nara—was inconsolable. My wife embraced her, and I placed in her small, calloused hand a genuine silver dollar, as a valued keepsake. Her giddy laughter (for Mara-Nara, laughter replaced tears) haunts me still.

Charlie stopped reading and tried to sleep again. He knew that the less he slept, the worse he'd feel, and that people were already looking at him as if something was wrong. Charlie recognized the signs: as with an election defeat or a fatal illness, everyone knew that you wouldn't be around much longer and began to act as if you'd already left. Abigail had once said, "When people lose in this town it's like they die. But they don't get buried and rot like real dead people; they stick around, and everybody hopes they leave." Charlie had replied that she must be in an awfully foul mood to say such things.

He still spent considerable time in front of a mirror, retying a tie, combing his graying hair. He'd begun to notice that his nose and cheeks had gotten redder, his expression more apprehensive, and that a kind of flabbiness had overtaken his upper body, which he blamed on the extra Scotch or so that he had each night. It had become harder to concentrate on legal work, and there seemed suddenly to be less of it.

In the evenings Charlie would return promptly to R Street, as if someone were waiting for him. He ate very little, had the Scotch, and tried to sleep before ten. The house already showed little evidence of someone else ever having lived there, apart from the dead brown ficus in the corner of the living room (Charlie had meant to toss it out, but something always made him hesitate: the finality of it) and some clothing in a guest room closet that Eve had intended to give away. Charlie often forgot to open the blinds in the morning and left most of the lights off at night; he knew that if he were watching someone else behaving this way, he would advise that person to get help. Outside he often heard dogs barking and their owners shouting and the dash of rats past the garbage cans in alleyways. When he thought how everything had been going badly for him, he also realized how things might get worse.

. . .

ANTHONY "PETE" THINGELD'S SKIN was so dry that it looked baked onto his fine bones, and his moist blue eyes seemed bigger. As Charlie took a seat, the last living founder of Thingeld, Pine & Sconce sat in his jurist's chair behind a moderately historic desk and scratched his head, then brushed the loose dandruff off the shoulders of his dark suit. Eventually he leaned forward, pity radiating from his watery eyes. Then he tilted back in his high-backed chair and sighed.

"Charlie," he said, "You need to deal with what I believe is a genuine problem area."

Charlie crossed his legs, feeling a little queasy. This was not what he'd come to hear. When he'd walked through the elevator doors this morning and nodded to everyone, he'd hoped that Pete would chuckle and pat his back and tell him to take a vacation. He stared for a moment at the photographic image of young Anthony as a member of the Princeton rowing team. Next to that he saw a family camping trip, two boys clambering over a supine, grinning Thingeld, whose head was resting on a canoe and whose hand was held by his wife, at the time an athletic woman with short blond hair.

"The problem is, I don't know what's going on," Charlie said, crossing his legs in the opposite direction.

Thingeld looked at his visitor as if he were examining an interesting specimen.

"Charlie," he said, scolding slightly, "I'm going ahead with this conversation on the presumption that you've done nothing wrong." He licked his lips and leaned forward again.

Charlie was surprised at what seemed to be a lingering question. "Well, Pete, that's true. And as a member of this firm, I have to agree that something needs to be cleared up. But I think it's something you may have started without meaning to."

"Charlie," Thingeld said sadly, slowly, "you're not part of this firm. You've left the firm." He paused and shook his head. "Believe me, Charlie, you've left us."

At that the queasy feeling returned, and Charlie had the sensation of slipping into a wormhole that would deposit him, penniless, in another planetary system.

"Of course technically you never formally resigned, and you might therefore have some claim against us," Thingeld continued. "But don't forget, you're not a partner but of counsel, as we agreed when you came on board. I rather hope we can settle this between gentlemen."

Charlie was alarmed by the contempt that he had just spotted in Thingeld's wet eyes.

"Your White House job—what a pity that didn't work out," Thingeld went on, shifting in his high chair. "It sounded perfect! But you know, Charlie, my experience is that whatever goes around comes around." Thingeld attempted a smile and his lips trembled. "You don't want to end up like me, Charlie," he said. "You may think I'm sitting pretty, but I know better."

He got up and held out his hand to the former congressman and, now, former member of Thingeld, Pine & Sconce.

"It isn't just me, Charlie," the senior partner continued, his hand still out. "There are women around here who get nervous when you walk through the door. You know, it hasn't helped matters that your wife just left you—your second wife. What's driving them away, Charlie? People are sympathetic of course, but they want to know that you're getting treatment for your problems. According to the people in our benefits office, the ones who see your medical claims, you're not getting any help at all."

Charlie stared at the senior partner, waiting for the signal that this was a joke, but there was no change in Thingeld's expression. When Charlie stood up, he felt almost dizzy. His voice rose a bit when he said, "Pete, that's something you made up. We're not talking about *me* now. *There is no problem.* You *invented* it!"

"If you were getting proper treatment, you wouldn't be facing all this," the founding partner replied, unmoved by Charlie's logic. "As I said, I doubt that your shapely young wife would have walked out if you were all right up here." Thingeld tapped his head.

Charlie's nausea swelled as he stared at Thingeld's outstretched hand and clasped it finally in a quick shake. He swallowed with great difficulty and then left hastily, rushing through the closing door of the elevator. He was blessedly alone when, as he began his downward glide, he vomited onto the carpeted floor. As he reached the street and bent to wipe off a tiny spot from a shoe, he thought about what sort of action plan he could devise for the rest of his life.

TWENTY

Not long after the dogwood blossoms withered, Pete Thingeld told Judith Grust that she'd been voted a partnership, and as he spoke about her brilliant future with Thingeld, Pine, he gripped her hand and seemed unable to wrap it up. Judith was very pleased—her promotion had come more than a year ahead of schedule—and she liked the way the other associates gave her envious looks. She got her hair done and went to Garfinckel's to buy expensive summer clothes. At the same time she was not as pleased as she thought she ought to be, perhaps because of a lingering uneasiness, a vague worry that, she supposed, had something to do with what she had done to Charlie Dingleman. Sometimes, when she tried to recall why precisely she'd reacted as she had, she couldn't remember his crime, apart from letting loose a hateful insult, right to her face, although she may have misunderstood even that; after all, he had been smiling almost meekly, as if he'd been attempting a joke. Perhaps she'd just been in a bad mood? Impossible!

When she heard that Charlie had been let go, she felt for the first time not only ashamed but almost depressed; it wasn't, she told herself, meant to go this far. Soon after Charlie left, Pete Thingeld, his cologne smelling of clove, had approached her by an office coffeepot, shaken his head, and whispered a worry that something tragic might befall their old comrade in arms. Judith sensed that

Thingeld, a spur of white hair flapping over his right ear, was looking at her with dread.

Judith also fretted about Hank Morriday. Now she was sorry that, more than once, she had let him into her bed, and into her, however clumsily and speedily. It was no casual matter to Judith; she could not understand those women who seemed to fuck (she spat the word in her mind) everyone they met, dancers in search of a perpetual pas de deux. She supposed that this made her a little stuffy, but she knew that grisly viruses could spurt from any man and that it was lunacy to take risks when the only reward was a moment of pleasure. There was no guarantee of that moment either.

Judith had hated running into Hank with that tough-looking woman from Big Tooth, Candysomething; it was as if they'd been on a date, just as it must have looked as if she'd been on a date with Alfred Schmalz. She realized that Hank and Candysomething could hurt her, a possibility that was more unsettling because of Judith's changing relationship (if that was the word) with Alfred Schmalz.

After the winter holidays the Schmalz family had surrounded her. Alfred Schmalz's daughter, Sylvia, called to ask about her father's mood. "I love it that Daddy is seeing you," Sylvia said. "He looks ten years younger when he's with you." Alfred Schmalz's sister, whose name was also Sylvia, invited Judith to shop with her at Garfinckel's and managed to say three times that Judith was rejuvenating her brother.

Such disclosures did not delight Judith, who suspected that the truth lay elsewhere: that she looked ten years older than the thirty-one she'd recently become. Back in January, on the night of the Schmalz family's post–New Year's dinner in Potomac, she had felt almost freakish in their company, closely watched behind a veil of lifted cutlery. After the meal, with the odor of roast beef clinging to him, Alfred had walked Judith from his fourteen-room house to her car and, steam escaping above his slightly discolored lip, suddenly staked a proprietary claim on her cheek. All she could do was smile when he stared with his mournful eyes.

At the law firm Schmalz would more often linger at Judith's office, trailing wordy pleasantries, closing the polished door gently behind him, as if by accident, always apologizing for the interruption. Wrapped in a three-piece dark wool suit, he would sit in the chair that faced her desk, cross a short leg and talk about his vision of the next generation. "What matters most to me are our young people, people like you who are struggling to find meaning in a world that seems ever more baffling," he said more than once, and when he had the opportunity, he would pat the back of her thin hand with his thick fingers.

Judith still thought he was the saddest man she'd ever known and wished he would do something about those dark suits and starched white shirts, the way his thin, gray hair was plastered across his head, those sorrowful eyes. She also wished that he would do something about his fatherly smile and repeated encouragements, especially when he said, "You have just a first-class mind, Judy." She was not always comfortable with the rest of Alfred Schmalz, the way he touched her hand, the next attempt to kiss her cheek behind a closed door (she had pulled away), the first hints that he sought more than mere friendship, the invitations to lunch at his club. Whenever he told Judith that she reminded him of his dead wife, she could not look at him. "I miss her less when I'm with you," he'd said in the spring, as tulips rose. "Does that make you uncomfortable? If so, I apologize; I would do nothing to make you uncomfortable. But I also want you to know what I'm feeling, and I want you to believe that it makes me happy to know that another person understands."

As Judith assured him that she did not object to such confidences, she noticed that his sad eyes were looking hungrily at her. When she was honest with herself, she supposed that there probably was not a great difference between Alfred Schmalz, the venerated partner, and Charlie Dingleman, the unpleasant, unemployed former congressman.

TWENTY-ONE

O NE BRIGHT APRIL MORNING on Massachusetts Avenue Hank
Morriday saw four men who looked like Dean Acheson. They had
small white mustaches, shiny black shoes, and pinstriped suits; when
Hank spied his own reflection in a window, he saw an anarchic
beard with gray streaks and a wrinkled cotton suit, a sight to make
him grimace. The real Dean Acheson, no matter how dead he had
become, was inseparable from a certain kind of Washington, a city
of bony couples and private clubs, of heated excitement (especially
in wartime)—a place that never quite welcomed someone like
Hank. The real Dean Acheson, he thought, would have been at a
table that bubbled with sober gaiety, a fluttering Perle Mesta, and
would not have let Candy Romulade lure him to a dreary meal with
a couple he did not quite know.

Sam and Melanie lived in Takoma Park (the Maryland side) in a
bungalow with low ceilings and large posters and broken toys
lodged under a brown sofa. Sam was a lawyer with the Federal
Trade Commission, where he and Candy had known each other,
and Melanie, also a lawyer, was with the Bureau of Fisheries. Their
daughters, five and seven, crawled onto their laps and plunged fingers into their dinner, a casserole, and then licked those fingers.

Candy had told Hank that Sam might get a "big job" in the next
administration—she'd heard that Dukakis consulted him about

antitrust issues—and Hank noticed that whenever Sam or Melanie uttered the word "Dukakis," it seemed to set off an internal signal for Candy to go outside and smoke. During one of these intervals Sam asked Hank how Candy was connected to the Dukakis campaign.

"That's our ulterior motive for asking you here," Sam said with a complicit smile.

Hank wasn't sure that he'd heard correctly. "Actually she told me that *you* were going to be doing something," he said.

Sam's fingernails were chewed away and his shiny black hair decorated a head that looked one size too large. Hank felt a noodle fall into his beard.

"Candy's the one with all the connections," said Melanie, whose eyes seemed to expand behind thick lenses.

"She's so great," Sam added, still smiling.

"Candy leads a fascinating life," Melanie said, not sensing Hank's confusion. "Such interesting clients. This country so desperately needs a change."

"There's a lot to be done," Sam added. "Antitrust policy is something I care deeply about."

"Sam keeps threatening to go into private practice, he's so disillusioned," Melanie said. "You can't believe what's happening with freshwater fish," she added, and mentioned an ex-congressman, Charlie something-or-other, whose record had been particularly scary.

Hank kept nodding as the conversation turned to polluted air, bigmouth bass, immigrants, public schools, and Ronald Reagan, and he began to fidget as Melanie brushed away a daughter who pulled at her skirt. When Candy returned, white smoke was leaking from her nostrils.

"Sam and Melanie are counting on your help," Hank said, very deliberately, to Candy. "With Dukakis," he added, satisfied at the disappointment that spread across Candy's face.

The evening went slowly. When Melanie smiled at him and said, "Hank, tell me just what it is you're working on," his mind froze. He knew that he bored people when he talked about the working poor or unemployables or cycles of dependency, but lately he'd begun to bore himself, hearing his own sentences trail off. Melanie's magnified eyes beamed at him and Hank was frantic to leave. He considered rushing to the bathroom, where he would go so far as to simulate the sound of retching.

"By the way, something about you seems very familiar," Melanie said to Hank, as her five-year-old with a determined look began to pull at her blouse. "I've been wanting to say that all evening. I just know I've seen you, or heard your name."

Hank was finding it harder to look at her—the way her enlarged eyes examined him. "Perhaps," he said, looking down, "on television?"

"No, it's not that. I never watch television. Television is stupid. Yes, *stupid!*" she added, when her child protested.

Then, as if she'd read his mind, Candy said, "You know, I promised Hank an early evening; he's just getting over a bug."

"I don't think I'm contagious," Hank assured them, with a glance at the seven-year-old, from whose mouth a fragment of noodle drooped. "But."

This took a little while, but soon enough the four of them were standing by the open doorway, shaking hands and expressing pleasure with the evening.

"You know we'd love to work for the governor," Melanie said. "We both believe in what he believes in."

"I'd like to hear more of his thoughts about antitrust," Sam said. "I'm afraid we're all going to be gobbled up."

"Life goes two ways, Sam," Candy replied.

Quite suddenly Melanie peered carefully at Hank and said, "I went to law school with Judith Grust. In Cambridge."

"Ah," Hank said, as Melanie watched him as if through a microscope.

"Judith is getting married, I hear," Melanie said.

. . .

HANK HAD FERRIED Candy to Takoma Park, and she was happy to let him drive her home. As they pulled away, she lit a cigarette, and as he shifted gears, she stroked the back of his cool hand with her warm fingers and smiled in a stiff way. "Sorry I dragged you to such an awful evening," she said, hunched slightly over the dashboard. "I'll take you to something fun soon to make up for it. I promise." She squeezed his hand.

Hank was startled by that affectionate gesture and thrilled by it too. He squeezed back and drove as quickly as he could through the city, which was so still that it seemed depopulated. The city made him nervous. When they were suddenly encircled by all sorts of urban blight, he shook his head sadly, then rolled up every window and locked the car's doors with a loud thump.

Candy lived in Virginia, just over the river, in a ten-story building with lots of parking. "I know it's a little sterile, but it has many amenities," Candy said when they arrived, and as they left the car, she exchanged neighborly nods with a man and woman who wore jogging shorts and huge tennis shoes and had very large, tanned calves. Then she stopped suddenly, and Hank saw that she was staring at a man with a pale face who stood next to a parked sedan. She shook her head, muttered, "Jesus!" and took Hank's hand. "Don't ask," Candy said, and Hank held her hand all the way upstairs and into her apartment.

As Candy went to hear what the answering machine had gathered up, Hank looked out a window, onto a swimming pool that was occupied by a few splashing singles. He flopped upon her pale blue sofa, all the pillows neatly arranged, and closed his eyes. On a side table he saw a copy of *My Four Trouble Spots*, which was showing up all over the place.

Hank heard the chorus of the answering machine. One voice belonged to Suzanne Smule, whose giggle seemed out of character. Another was from someone at Big Tooth, who was saying something about a guest list for the "Reynolds Mund gala." The last voice sounded a little desperate, and Hank tried to make out each muffled word. "It's me," that voice said. "Martin. I'm just calling to ask if you've seen Teresa." A pause. "Well, I guess you're not there."

Candy came back while Hank was looking at the photographs on a small writing desk: Candy shaking hands with Jimmy Carter, signed in blue ink "with very best wishes"; Candy with her stern-looking parents; Candy at a Big Tooth party, her arms around the woman who shared her office, who was wearing an Orioles cap. "I see you're looking at my past," Candy said. She moved closer to Hank, and she leaned against him wearily. "My better past," she added.

"I know," Hank said, and put his arm now around her, gripping her below the shoulder. "You miss being at the center of things."

Candy looked at him a little doubtfully. "I miss making a difference," she said. "I try to make a difference, but the truth is I work with assholes. They don't trust me to do anything right."

"What's wrong with them?" Hank asked.

Candy wished that he wouldn't scratch her neck with his beard when he spoke.

"I really screwed up," she said. "You know, that congressman I told you about."

Candy saw herself in a mirror; her face, she thought, looked far too old for her body, and she was almost surprised that anyone wanted to kiss her.

"It's good to make a difference," Hank said, his beard brushing her ear. "It's very good. It's what I think about when I think about intractable problems. But something keeps driving me to try to solve them."

Candy did not wholly trust Hank, but as she became unwrapped, the air thick with blue cushions, she stopped listening to him. There was Hank Morriday, somewhat breathless, revealing an enormous pink birthmark on his belly like a great planetary ring, the freckles like tiny asteroids, and a blemish at the side like a dark comet invading the inner solar system. As Candy pulled him into her bedroom, her thoughts were elsewhere. Later, as they lay side by side (Hank appeared unusually content) and the telephone rang like an alarm, Candy pulled away speedily.

"Look," she was saying, "I don't know what I can do to help." Silence. "I don't *know* where she goes, but I can't control her." Her voice had a tense shrillness. "What makes you think I can? She's not *my* wife."

Hank got up and looked out Candy's largest window, the one that faced Washington, across the river, toward the obelisk and its marble companions. He stared down at the water until all he could see were the pale reflections of light from the tiny imperial city. "Get hold of yourself, Martin," Candy told her caller. "If you can't get hold of yourself, no one else can do it for you. You scared me just before, outside." Candy paused, as if to catch her breath, and lit a cigarette. "Okay, tell you what," she was saying. "If I hear anything, I'll call you." She paused. "Yes, yes, that's a promise."

As Hank half-listened to Candy's baffling dialogue, he thought of people across the Potomac: of his doppelganger Crane and Suzanne Smule, of friends who'd gotten married and called him less and less, of Sam and Melanie, of Judith Grust and Candy Romulade and Dean Acheson, and of all the mischief the city made in places far away. He looked toward the southeast and northeast quadrants, where the lights were not so bright, and thought about his unwritten book. When Candy saw Hank at the window, his puffy buttocks uncovered, his head slightly bowed, she had the alarming thought that she wanted to be someplace else forever.

.   .   .

AT ABOUT THE TIME that Hank Morriday, with virile triumph, was saying good night to Candy Romulade, Teresa Maracopulos was at the television station. It was nearly midnight, and Reynolds Mund was restless, as he often was after a broadcast. He had changed into an open-necked plaid shirt, the sleeves rolled up along his thin arms. Every time she visited the bright little newsroom, Teresa was fascinated—by the set and the people running about, the robot cameras, the fidgeting. Now everyone had left.

Teresa was pleased with herself. Because of her, Candy—her best work friend—had been asked to plan Reynolds Mund's anniversary celebration. Candy really owed her; they all did. Even Dennis had patted her shoulder with approval. And now she had every reason to spend more time with the anchorman.

Teresa liked to sit in the chair where he sat, his very spot for nearly twenty years; as she straightened her hair with her fingers, she could imagine being his coanchor. "That was a very moving story, Reynolds," she could hear herself saying. She knew that Martin would be worried about her. Several times she'd meant to call, but then she'd forget, or perhaps she just didn't want to talk to him. Martin had to learn, as he'd said so sarcastically, to give her space. When Teresa pointed out that she ought to be heading home—it was late—the anchorman asked her to stay a bit longer. He had something to show her, he said, and she followed him along a corridor, then down a narrow metal staircase.

"You'll like this," he said.

They came to a storeroom filled with sheets of plywood, many of them used for the sets of programs that were no longer on the air. One painted board looked like the altar of a church and on the other side was an automotive repair shop with a 1977 Dodge on a lift. Propped against that was the Capitol, used for a Sunday morning program where politicians were asked questions by locally famous reporters. Reynolds Mund was a little short of breath as he hurried past each panel, as if he was looking for something, as indeed he was.

A few minutes later he found it: painted on a slightly warped sheet of plywood were a red barn and yellow silo, the countryside looming behind it, and a white fence and grass that was startlingly green. Not far from the fence stood an udderless cow, its brown eyes watchful.

"They put this away when Ranger Joe got sick and died," the anchorman told her, and he got that faraway look. Then he sang: "'For Ranger Joe, it's time to go, but let's be partners again.'" His smile got crooked. "I loved that show," he said. "I learned a lot from it."

Teresa nodded. She vaguely remembered the Ranger Joe program. The anchorman meanwhile had opened a trunk marked "Ranger Joe," which was in a corner. He removed a white ten-gallon hat. "I'd like to wear this for the news," he said, his craggy grin springing out as he put on the hat.

"You should," Teresa said. Of course he was kidding her. Then she looked at her watch and said, "I should be leaving."

"Is your husband jealous of our time together?" the anchorman asked with an odd sort of smile. He'd asked that question before.

"It's just that it's late," Teresa said.

The anchorman, ignoring that declaration, lifted a pair of spurs, jingling them as he closed the trunk lid.

"I like to visit with Ranger Joe," he said, and he tried to attach the spurs to the backs of his soft loafers. For a few moments, wearing a big white hat and silvery spurs that wouldn't stay put, he looked not at all like a cowboy but rather like someone frail and possibly unwell, someone who couldn't possibly ride the range. "You know what else I like, don't you, Thelma?"

"Teresa," she said. She still got annoyed when he forgot her name. "And I know what you're going to say. You're going to talk about those silly news molecules again."

Reynolds Mund turned right around, his expression not at all friendly; he had the look that frightened her, the one where his face was like a dead sun, and she was suddenly a little afraid at being there alone with him.

"You're a stupid little girl," he said, and flung down his ten-gallon hat.

"But I'm learning," she replied, and she meant it.

TWENTY-TWO

In the short time that Judith Grust had anything to do with Hank Morriday, she sometimes felt as if some cosmic Chooser was overruling her silent objections and would lead them with a sure hand into marriage. They would live in Cleveland Park or Chevy Chase; their children would go to Sidwell or St. Albans; they would drive Volvo wagons in perfect safety, and in the summer they'd go where their friends went, to Wellfleet and the Vineyard; they would be Washingtonians of the race, class, and occupation that made up their worlds.

Sometimes she felt like calling Hank just to chat, to put any bad feelings behind them, to tell him the good news about herself. Often this impulse came after a day under the paper volcano of a Washington law firm or when she was on the exercise machine, wet with perspiration as her television showed pictures of mayhem from just around the corner, and she would see that what remained of her night were the documents—the depositions, affidavits, briefs, citations, precedents—she'd brought home, the frozen dinner that had looked so tasty in the supermarket, and the telephone inviting her to call her mother or a law school acquaintance like Melanie, who worked in the Bureau of Fisheries and was married to someone named Sam.

But Judith wanted more than a mere chat with Hank. She wanted to discuss their little scheme and what they—yes, *they*—might have done to Charlie Dingleman, who had dropped out of sight. Who would have thought that one telephone call could do such harm? Not her. True, she had wanted to keep Charlie away from the White House. But it wasn't, she swore to herself, meant to end this way.

One afternoon in April Judith called the Institute and left Hank a friendly, almost flirtatious message. ("Hi, it's really me. It's been too long, so give me a call.") The day had begun with a complicated probate case that Alfred Schmalz had handed her, saying, "I trust you more than anyone to sort this out." But she could not concentrate on the case, which involved a young widow whose grown-up stepchildren wanted everything (Thingeld, Pine represented the stepchildren), and when Hank did not return her call, she thought of his ragged beard, his studious eyes, and the pleasure he might take in ignoring her. She thought of going to his office or his apartment and shook her head at the idea of stalking Hank.

But when Hank didn't call back, as azaleas sprouted around the city like pink footnotes, Judith decided that she might need the advice of a lawyer, just in case; Hank's silence was worrisome. Was she overreacting, imagining plots—Hank & Candy!—against her? She knew that when one is exceedingly tired (the rings under her eyes had grown darker), one becomes irrational. But a good lawyer is always prepared for combat, and when she called Alfred Schmalz, he sounded joyful at the prospect of serving, however informally. "Judith," he said softly, "I'm sure you have no exposure, whatever your problem is, but it's never unwise to be too cautious, especially now that you're about to be a partner," and he urged her to come at once to his office.

In the room where Alfred Schmalz worked, hunched by his desk, he beckoned her to sit, his eyes rich with interest in her plight, now and then darting to her few inches of exposed thigh, or so Judith suspected; one could never be sure. She looked at him, then at relics of his past, all stridently visible: a portrait of his two Sylvias, a grin-ning grandson, a large photograph of himself leaning across a desk, his tie dangling as his forehead almost touched Dean Rusk's fore-head. The Schmalz with Rusk, Judith realized, was not much older than she herself; when she was in the second grade, Schmalz's words to Rusk were being frozen in mid-utterance. His dark three-piece suit looked just like the one he wore now.

"It must be very painful for you even to talk about this," Schmalz said, walking to Judith's side and resting his thick fingers on her shoulder. "I'm well aware, you know, of your history, and I imagine it has something to do with that."

What history? Judith tried to shrug away this weight, but it did not move; the hand rested softly in place, and a thumb tenderly stroked the side of her neck. Judith then reached up and plucked away this moving part.

"I'm sorry, Alfred, but that isn't comfortable for me," she said.

"You mean that it is uncomfortable?" he asked at once. "Or do you mean that you feel uncomfortable when I touch you in a friendly way? You draw from me all my protective, caring feelings, and nothing would hurt me more than to think that I have in some way crossed a line in the confusion of those emotions."

Alfred Schmalz returned to sit in the tall, dark red leather chair that loomed up behind his desk (taller than Thingeld's chair) and looked at Judith with eyes that seemed about to fill with tears. Judith sensed that this moment was important, that what she said next could affect her future; she also sensed that she should never have begun this and that it might be better for her to leave right away, al-though she didn't.

"I meant it was uncomfortable because my shoulder is sore from working out," Judith said, and an expression of happiness bloomed from the sad face of the senior partner.

Alfred Schmalz folded his hands in much the way that Pete Thingeld folded his, and as he did this, as his eyes darted again to Judith's legs, she made an important, perhaps reckless decision.

"You said something, Alfred, about knowing my history," she said, her head bowed, "so I have to ask you, as a friend and counselor, what you meant by that."

Schmalz's compassionate expression grew as if being inflated.

"As a senior partner I've got to be kept informed of these things, sometimes in more detail than any of us would wish," he said, and as Judith wondered how much he'd been told, he added that before they'd voted on her partnership, Pete had told him everything, although he'd been discreet. "My understanding is that poor Charlie Dingleman may have said things that made you very uncomfortable. That is bad enough, and we all deplore that, but I also understand that he may have done more, something too delicate for you to talk about."

Schmalz's eyes widened as he said this and in mid-phrase he licked his purplish lower lip. Judith, who did not know what to say, accepted this mysterious thesis; he was once more standing next to her and his fingers were again resting on a shoulder, massaging her gently.

"You seem so very, very tense, Judith," was the explanation. "I shan't hurt you this time."

Judith sighed; she would abide by her decision and tell her lawyer what she'd done. She placed her hand atop his and squeezed it as she would a harmless object.

"When it comes to Charlie Dingleman," she said, "I have not always behaved well myself."

Their hands remained bound as Judith, not looking at Alfred Schmalz, told him how she'd done something to ensure that the public life of Charlie Dingleman would end, although in the telling,

Judith gave Hank Morriday a far more active role than the one she'd assigned to herself; full confession, she instinctively understood, was bad for the career. "My friend Hank made the telephone call, and I can't deny that I may have encouraged it," she said. "But I really didn't think anything would happen. And I really think that I acted solely in the national interest. Who would want someone unstable in such a sensitive office?" As she spoke, hearing her own voice as if from a distance, Alfred Schmalz's soft right hand moved to her neck, which he stroked softly, a sensation that Judith found not unpleasant, although she wished the hand were not now finding its way down her back to the clasp of her brassiere and that his ring were not so cold. She knew that she should not permit this.

"As your lawyer," Alfred Schmalz said, "I can only advise you to tell no one. As someone who is pleased to think of himself as your mentor, I can only say that I'm proud of you for having the courage to tell me this. As I understand it, you were acting out of patriotism; his public career concerned you, not his sad professional one. You saw his hand next to the hand that's on the button." Schmalz's hand rubbed her back under her blouse, finding the clasp it sought, as she agreed with his analysis.

Judith found his hand strangely uncertain in its journey, and she became aware that he was breathing more heavily and that there was movement within his dark trousers, inches away. For a moment, she let her head drop, a gesture of trust and relaxation, as his hand stroked on, circling the clasp on her back but doing nothing to unfasten it. She told him to stop what he was doing and then realized that she had not quite said those words aloud.

"You have a brilliant future here," Alfred Schmalz continued, stopping to breathe deeply. "You have a quick mind, an amazing grasp of complex legal issues, especially"—a *click!* as he undid the clasp—"for someone of your age; it's why I recommended you for the fast track. I speak this way, Judy, I hope you know, as someone who has become inordinately fond of you, seeing in you a person about to blossom on her own and also someone who reminds me of another person I miss more than words can say."

What was he doing now? Judith felt his thick hand as it tried to find a shortcut to a breast (it was past her arm and not far from the tip of one) and she heard the unmistakable sound of a zipper. When she opened her eyes, she saw that the vertical passageway in Alfred Schmalz's dark trousers led to a red blaze of boxer shorts.

"Take it," he whispered to her, "in your hand." Judith felt as if she might throw up. "Please," he said, and with his other hand led her thin fingers to their swollen destination. "Please," he said again, in a whispery moan.

Judith, her eyes closed, grasped the familiar part, thinking that it felt much the same as Hank Morriday's, rubbing it as she'd done with that boy she'd gone out with in ninth grade, whatever his name, her fingers gliding and squeezing just enough to make him hers entirely. But when she felt the spasm within her fist and he took away her hand, murmuring thanks, she thought that it had to have been someone else who had just done that.

"You must also," Alfred Schmalz was saying sadly, holding a handkerchief before him as he retreated to his desk, "learn to forgive a man his weaknesses."

Judith looked into his reddened face without forgiveness. Outside the window spring light filled K Street and the brightness of it dazzled Judith as hatred passed through her like a convulsion.

"How could you make me do that?" she said, feeling inspired—as she'd felt in other rooms with other men—knowing that the words she'd chosen were just the right ones to bring fear to his pained eyes.

Alfred Schmalz shook his head and bowed it so that Judith could see his pink, dry scalp under his matted gray hair. "Because I love you," he said.

Tears filled Judith's eyes, and when she said to him that the time would come when she'd want a favor too, a very large favor, her cheeks were still wet. As Alfred Schmalz nodded, she could see that the kindness that had suffused his face was disappearing like a cloud.

TWENTY-THREE

Although Martin Himmelschaft had grown up in Washington, he rarely felt at home. He supposed that this happened to others: the older you got, the more you left the city of your youth. In Martin's case that city was Washington in 1955: an imperfect square, a place where tourists photographed outsized monuments and Rock Creek Park was safe. Now that Martin was forty-five and the woman he adored no longer seemed to need him, he tried to recover his past. He did this by ignoring whatever disturbed it.

In 1955, when Martin was twelve, the Washington Senators played seventy-seven baseball games a year in Griffith Stadium—players like Wayne Terwilliger and Clyde Kluttz, on a scruffy field. Now there was no Griffith Stadium and no baseball and these absences angered Martin, enough to make him silently shake his fist whenever he drove south along Georgia Avenue. In 1955 streetcars wobbled through the city and into the nearby countryside; a twelve-year-old could wander fearlessly and people spoke in a nasal variation of a mid-South dialect. Now Martin's city was surrounded by tens of thousands of cars speeding past the cube-shaped buildings of software consultants and defense contractors, filled with people from elsewhere. Not that his childhood had been altogether peaceful; now and then Martin had gotten into terrible rages, and once he'd thrown a large rock at a friend that (the memory was still disturbing) might have permanently damaged his friend.

Martin Himmelschaft's father had been an analyst with the Bureau of Standards, and although Martin never quite knew what his father did for a living (or why there should be a Bureau of Standards), he discovered that other people nodded knowingly when it came up. In 1955 Martin's father sometimes took his wife and son downtown to Barkley's, where young Martin stared at Walter Johnson's uniform and once saw John Foster Dulles excitedly waving a fork at a dinner companion. After 1955 Martin grew up. He left home and went to the University of Maryland, stayed to get a master of science degree, and took a job with the D.C. government, where he'd never planned to stay but was now three years short of his twenty-fifth year in the personnel office. He no longer went to Barkley's, which was patronized by the sort of people who got bored by people like Martin; it was ironic, he thought, that Teresa Maracopulos, who actually was born in 1955, would ask him to take her there. She had not seemed interested when he'd pointed to the life-sized, cold-eyed wax figure of John Foster Dulles and told her that long ago he'd seen the real thing.

"Those people aren't your friends, Teresa," Martin said more than once. "What do you get out of being with them?"

Martin still remembered her look of baffled horror when she replied, "This has to do with being in this fabulous city in this amazing time in our history. And I've got to tell you, I don't appreciate it when you try to take my fun away." She paused and added, "I think it's because you don't ever have any fun yourself, stuck with all those drones."

He was hurt; she was referring to his pals from high school, with whom he still played poker, and to the people in his office, who could be lots of fun, and to the "O's Folks," who took a bus to Orioles games once a month. But he was the one who apologized. Then he stopped himself from saying how he hated to see her wearing that jewelry—the silver pin of two big teeth biting into the globe. He did say, "I do have fun, Teresa," knowing that she couldn't imagine it. "I wish you'd come to a ball game once in a while."

In the weeks that he'd realized something was wrong between them, Martin was feeling older and wearier. That affected his appearance, and everyone saw it when he showed up for work in his cream-and-brown office. Ginny Lou, the chubby black woman in the cubicle next to his, was starting to look concerned when she poked in her head and said, "How's it going, baby?" Martin believed that if he were to be hit by a bus, the world would not mourn one less administrator in the city personnel office, but he still replied, "Hey, Ginny Lou, you look hot today."

Martin felt curiously jealous when Teresa headed off each day to Big Tooth. He knew how she still affected men, the way they crowded around her in public places, for that was how she still affected him. He worried whenever she told him about meeting a Big Tooth client, many of whom seemed sinister, resembling in Martin's imagination Yasser Arafat. He worried when she was out of the office and Candy Romulade, her officemate and friend, could not (or would not) tell him where she was, and she'd been away a lot.

The Washington that Martin had known in 1955 was a city that people like Candy Romulade could never have imagined. Or so Martin sometimes told himself when he rode the Metro back to their two-bedroom townhouse on Fifteenth Street, Northeast, and tried not to notice the bullet holes in nearby bricks or, once, the splayed body of someone who'd been shot and who gave one last groan and died before the cops showed up.

He worried that such a thing might happen to Teresa, which was why he always told her to be careful. He thought more about moving; that was all the neighbors talked about, each one knowing the price of every house sold within three blocks. The brightly colored

Victorian row houses, several of which had For Sale signs in their tiny front yards, made him think of a tranquil, slightly homicidal village. Martin thought that if he sold it now, he'd get back nine thousand dollars or so of the fourteen thousand down payment, and when you thought about losing five thousand, it didn't sound so bad, and maybe some of it could be a tax deduction. Or so Martin Himmelschaft thought when he couldn't get to sleep and wasn't thinking of Teresa's new habits, such as always wanting to watch the eleven o'clock news.

. . .

ONE WARM EVENING (the night that Hank and Candy visited Sam and Melanie), when Martin had come home and couldn't reach Teresa, he had felt something close to panic. Remote thunderstorms rattled the air, and when he couldn't even get hold of Candy Romulade, he had driven to Virginia, looping about until he found Candy's building. By the time he'd pulled into a guest parking spot, he wasn't quite sure why he'd done it; several times he had stopped at telephone booths to call home, hoping that Teresa might finally be back. Martin was about to return across the Potomac when he had spotted Candy walking toward the lobby. She had been accompanied by a man in a seersucker suit, a fellow of about forty, a schmuck, Martin judged, from the supercilious knot of his beard. From his car he could see Candy's thin, tanned face, smoke gushing from her nose, and the silver pin on her dress. She made the tip of her cigarette burn hotly and tugged at the arm of the schmuck; after they disappeared into the lobby, Martin had watched the enlarging shapes of jet planes approaching the airport and saw in the distance the spooky tip of the Monument.

A little later, when Martin called from a phone booth nearby, Candy had said, "You have to learn to let go," showing off her mastery of the American tongue.

"What the fuck is happening to my wife?" he had asked.

"You don't seem to understand her real needs," Candy had said. "I know that hurts, Martin, but it's the truth."

Martin believed then that Candy Romulade was not his friend and that she knew much more than she would tell him. He felt himself losing control, getting worked up into a rage.

TWENTY-FOUR

B Y MAY Hank Morriday noticed that more people at the Institute were taking longer lunches, returning to shut their doors in what appeared to be very private meetings—activity, he was sure, directed at finding jobs in the new administration, which was forming with cell-like haste. He imagined the Massachusetts governor calling people like Suzanne Smule, eager planets orbiting this chilly sun, and he saw himself as a lost comet, an icy dwarf, racing toward the Kuiper Belt. He would have dreams that ended with him crying, "Wait for me!"

Somewhat to his surprise, Hank was becoming attached to Candy Romulade, even if she bit her knuckles and smoked her way through packs of cigarettes; he trusted her and watched with fondness whenever she raced to telephones at restaurants and gas stations to check messages. At such moments he would regard her slender legs and dark blond hair and sometimes imagine—hope—that she would turn out to be someone else, yet also be grateful when she didn't. Unlike Judith Grust, who by now had left two or three messages, Candy Romulade seemed actually to like him.

Candy continued to invite Hank to events, roomfuls of people that he'd seen in other rooms around the city. He went along because Candy wanted him to, but he dreaded the very smell of such occasions, like perfumed locker rooms, and he feared that he was becoming as watchful and uncertain as Candy, who spent much of her time putting together guest lists and then fretting that no one important would show up.

For Hank certain moments were worse than others, such as his first actual conversation with Crane. This took place on a warm night in a crowded room, when Hank and his doppelganger found themselves side by side, holding glasses of fizzless Perrier and placing mushroomlike food on tongues that flicked out from identical black beards, although Hank's beard was flecked with gray.

"I know we've met before," Crane said. "You were pointed out to me. Perhaps at the Institute?"

"I believe we're in the same field, and we're both there," Hank replied.

"Oh, right," Crane said. "You're writing something, isn't that so? Someone told me that, someone who pointed you out to me."

"I'm trying to remember where it was we met, but I remember that you were pointed out to me too," Hank said.

"And you're working on . . . ?"

"Comparative social welfare policy," Hank said, hearing a voice that sounded like the voice he used when he was being interviewed. "I'm studying our system and also postwar Europe's—the social democrats and all that." Hank paused and at that moment felt almost excited by his project. "Pretty interesting stuff, actually. I'm breaking new ground."

Crane gobbled a piece of food that had just arrived, a crescent shape, red and green, with something light brown oozing from its side. As he said something that Hank could not quite hear above the murmur, Hank was shoved from behind. Someone else he'd seen before, the woman who he thought was named Robin, who had shiny black hair and wore a thin, sleeveless blue dress, materialized and tugged at Crane's sleeve, letting loose a brilliant red smile, not noticing Hank. An instant later she kissed Crane's cheek, giving his beard a fiery smear.

"I try to keep the governor briefed on poverty," Crane said, turning to Hank, then to the sleeveless woman. "I'm telling him," he explained to her, apparently having already forgotten Hank's name, "how amazing Mike is. He has an almost superhuman ability—I don't know how else to put it—to absorb the implications of almost everything."

Robin nodded in quick assent and said, "He somehow grasps more than the rest of us."

Between sleeve aperture and shoulder, Hank tried not to stare at the swelling of a breast; whether it was in a brassiere was unclear, and for a second (until she looked at him with suspicion) he thought of trying to improve his angle of vision. He looked from Crane to the likely Robin and then with relief to Candy Romulade, who had suddenly joined their little circle, her face tense, perspiration bubbles below her nose.

"Are you working for Mike too?" Robin asked Hank.

He shrugged. "Not at this time," he said enigmatically.

"But you can count us as people who are trying to help," Candy said quickly, looking intently at Crane. "The fact that people like Hank and you, two of our leading theorists on welfare, care about this campaign makes me feel more hopeful."

Hank smiled at the woman whose name he thought was Robin and thought how very pretty she was. A waiter carrying the silver tray of red-and-green crescents walked by just out of reach, but Candy managed to snag one. At this moment Hank's doppelganger did not appear pleased, and as if to explain this mood, Robin (Hank now spotted a forlorn, dark blue brassiere strap) looked at Candy with some defiance.

"Actually," she said, "I would describe Crane as *the* leading theorist on poverty and welfare. People are in awe of him, and I don't think the governor would ever make a move without consulting him."

Crane smiled benignly from the depths of his beard.

"Don't exaggerate," he commanded.

The dark-haired woman kissed him again.

"I also love your modesty," she said, then turned to Hank with a look that made him feel that he had been sentenced to obscurity without parole. "It was very nice to meet you," she said, to which Hank said the same thing. When he turned the other way, he saw that his doppelganger had nearly disappeared, talking now to the bow-tied columnist Brandon Sladder. Candy Romulade's face became paler, frozen in pain, and the woman with no sleeves became a curious half smile.

"Let's get out of here," Candy Romulade whispered to Hank. "This is a lousy party, a very lousy party," she went on, glancing toward no one in particular. "There's a better event next week, a fundraiser for the governor. Some bimbo television star will be there," she added, and after Candy mentioned the star's name, Hank barely heard her murmur something about "this fucking job."

TWENTY-FIVE

CHARLES DINGLEMAN'S financial settlement from Thingeld, Pine would last only for a few lean months, yet he couldn't force himself to think about the future; the present was unsettling enough. He felt mildly embarrassed if he spotted someone he recognized and usually turned away, as if to become invisible; even strangers, he supposed, were judging him, much as the voters of Pennsylvania had, and seemed to believe that he was a man with mysterious, deviant habits.

One day just as he opened his knee-high iron gate to the sidewalk, he saw the journalist's widow, who must have just acquired that terrier with the red collar and long whiskers. She turned with a quavering smile as if she hadn't heard what everyone else in town seemed to know.

"You don't remember me?" she asked, as her black terrier urinated against his fence. "We met long ago, when my husband was still alive, and we talked in Dumbarton Oaks." She glanced affectionately at her new dog.

"Of course I do," Charlie replied.

"Perhaps we also met at the Dobsons'?" she asked, her eyebrows lifted, referring to one of the most venerated families on Q Street. "You've heard about their cat, I imagine?"

Charlie nodded again, though he hadn't a clue who the Dobsons were or the status of their cat, which he presumed was the hissing and scratching breed. Then she said, "I'm sorry about your difficulties," and her eyes were alarmingly wide with interest in his life.

. . .

CHARLIE BEGAN TO SPEND too much time alone. For a few days he thought that the coiled telephone cord looked like a snake, silent and ready to pounce, and one morning he kicked the phone across the room, which made its ring faint and sputtering and wrecked his answering machine. No doubt that was why he missed hearing from Abigail, who later told him that she'd repeatedly called to remind him that their daughter was about to graduate from Tufts. When Abigail finally did reach him and Charlie realized that he'd actually missed the ceremonial day, he felt a shiver of mortification and then a kind of terror. Nothing, he thought, should change; constancy was all, and yet the opposite was always true.

"That was pretty unforgivable," Abigail said.

"I'd love to see you," Charlie replied in agony. "I almost called you quite a few times. It's been ages."

"I know it's been very hard for you personally," she said, "but that's no excuse."

"I'll call Jessica right away," he said.

"I do think it's outrageous, the things they've said about you," she said. "So does James."

"Maybe we could get together," he said.

"James sells real estate too," she said. "Millions of dollars a year."

"For a drink or something," Charlie said, but Abigail said that she didn't want to encourage his drinking.

. . .

AS THE HOT SEASON BEGAN, as the air took on the sweet foulness that became the scent of the late twentieth century, Charlie went to a retirement party for a CIA man. He'd apparently been invited by mistake (the invitation had gone to his old congressional office and been forwarded), but he went anyway. The spy lived in a Potomac, Maryland, subdivision in a brand-new brick house the size of a palace; and as soon as Charlie walked across a bright green lawn and circular driveway and shook the hand of the CIA man's small, quiet wife (about sixty years old, he guessed; she had an unlined face and wore a checked cotton dress), he found that a curious space formed around him. It was not that the other guests were avoiding him but that they seemed always to be on the other side of the enormous, freshly painted rooms, stumbling across the Early American–style furniture, getting out of his way at a black marble wet bar, swatting flies. Charlie recognized quite a few people from his time on the Hill, and he walked swiftly in circles, drink in hand, until he spotted Fred Hykler, his former neighbor and best friend in Congress, who had not returned his calls in weeks.

"Charlie, my man! Where you been keeping yourself?" Fred asked with a worried expression. He peered first over Charlie's head and then across each shoulder, nodding silent greetings to men—all the guests were men—some of whom Charlie could not see. Fred had a streak of California sunburn between his hair and eyebrows; Charlie thought that his perspiring nose looked large and veiny, and he enjoyed the sight of that flawed feature.

"Fred!" Charlie replied with booming bonhomie. "You're a tough fellow to get hold of."

Hykler chuckled in the way that he'd learned to chuckle when he was asked an uncomfortable question and said, "I know it's been rough, Charlie, and I've meant to call. I've had to spend a lot of time on the Coast—got to take these elections seriously."

Charlie was grateful for these untruths as Hykler chuckled again, his small dark eyes drifting elsewhere, his hand sending yet another signal to a distant part of the room, getting a wave from a rosy-cheeked expert in military intelligence who gripped a plate piled high with food. "Hey," he said, "do you think our man Bush can pull this off?"

Charlie had been paying little attention to the fortunes of his party. "Some people think it's a Democratic year," he said gravely. "Not good for Poppy."

Fred Hykler, he could see, was fidgeting.

"How's the wife?" Charlie asked, as if their conversation were just beginning. "It's been a while, Fred, but let me tell you: after a time you realize there *is* life after Congress."

The torment on the face of his former best friend made it clear that Fred could not stand another minute of Charlie's company. "I see Abigail now and then," Fred said. "She looks swell. She seems real happy in fact." He looked down, then up. "I haven't said hello to the guest of honor," he added, gesturing toward the retiring CIA man, who was limping stiffly toward the bar.

"Me neither," Charlie said, sticking close.

The retiring spy had a prosthesis below his right knee, and a hearing aid filled one ear; his thin head was shaved. There was a story that he'd been injured in a car bombing in Manila, or an ambush in Athens, or by a sniper in Saigon, stories that the retiring spy had taken care to spread. The truth was that he'd had his leg crushed by a bus in London because he'd forgotten to look to his right after leaving a topless bar in Soho. He seemed to know just when Charlie and Fred Hykler were behind him.

"Congrats," Fred Hykler said, holding out his hand.

"Me too," Charlie said, extending his too.

"Fred, how kind of you," the retiring spy said, raising his eyebrows. Then to Charlie, whom he did not seem to know, he asked, "Have you met my wife?" shoving him gently in the direction of the whitened figure of the only woman in the house. In that instant Fred Hykler made his escape.

Charlie helplessly shook her limp, chilly hand.

"It's so awful," she said, "about that Iranian airplane," and Charlie nodded, surprised to hear her talking about the passenger plane that had been shot down by mistake.

"All those bodies in the water," he said carefully, remembering the sight of them and shapeless bits of clothing floating across his silent television screen.

"Mistakes get made," she said, and then she too turned away, leaving Charlie once more enclosed by the peculiar wall behind which he faded from view.

TWENTY-SIX

J UDITH GRUST WORRIED about the face she saw reflected in the ladies' lounge at Thingeld, Pine & Sconce (that weariness, those shoots of gray hair), but she was glad that she would have lots more prestige and lots more money, although she was not quite sure how she'd spend it all. Alfred Schmalz had been urging her to buy a place outside the District, in a neighborhood like his with twelve-speed bicycles and overstocked grocery stores. He was quick to point out what happened to those who stayed in the city: people got hurt; savagery was rife. He wasn't a prejudiced man—quite the contrary!— but he had to say that the blacks were out of control. And that mayor! Judith got used to the soft repetitions of these arguments, but she could not get used to her own altered aspect. For four days straight she shopped for clothes, choosing colors to make herself look younger and softer, although no less serious. She began to read women's magazines (so much about orgasms and making men happy by understanding their sex organs) as she peered over the calendar's edge to view the childless beyond.

More than hard work affected Judith's appearance, although the work never stopped: she could not get away from the brick-colored legal folders and unanswered messages. It was a feeling of woe, which even the prospect of earning more than $150,000 a year did not diminish. Judith knew that she didn't deserve to feel this way. She was not, she knew, a bad person, even if she'd done some bad things; she was merely human. But Judith understood that by accepting her early partnership, she had assumed a kind of debt to Alfred Schmalz, and that this canceled out his debts to her. When the gloomy Schmalz visited her office, closed the door, and smiled sadly, the subject of her confession didn't come up; he would usually talk about anything else, often beginning a monologue about the misdeeds of the Reagan administration and how important it was for young people not to lose faith in the system. Or he would tell her about a play he had seen in New York or some unusual accomplishment of his precocious grandson. Now and then as he talked about art, politics, and the law, he might hover so close that he'd brush against her, his pink-red Hermès tie flapping at her hair. Sometimes she would get up, but eventually (how she loathed him!) she'd gone ahead and unzipped and held him wrapped between her fingers, his discolored lip tremulous until he was done and he could begin his apologies anew, although recently she'd heard him whisper something about using her mouth.

"You must forgive me my weakness," he would say to Judith, as perspiration gave his face a fresh sheen. "I know you despise me when I'm like this, but humanity survives because we try to help each other as we move through our days on this planet. Rusk used to say something like that in our darkest moments."

If Judith was unswayed, Alfred Schmalz would elaborate on the benefits—a Christmas bonus, a 401k, tickets to Redskins games— quite apart from what lower-tier partners made (although nothing could be taken for granted; it was important to find new clients). Judith, clenching her teeth, would let him touch her shoulder, his thin gold wristwatch spangling as he offered his hand in marriage, which she needed to think over, or so she said with averted eyes.

Judith supposed that someday she would have to punish Alfred Schmalz for the truly unforgivable way that he'd sought to amortize her debt, yet she did not want him as an enemy when really it took so little to keep him on her side; she expended fewer calories on him than she would merely climbing onto her exercise machine. Also she was never sure what Alfred Schmalz was really thinking and whether, although she was sure he'd never intentionally do anything to hurt her, he might take some pleasure in frightening her. There were, after all, those few times when he would fixate her with his acutely sad brown eyes and tell her things that made her anxious—rumors and such—like the fact that Pete Thingeld had asked him whether Judith might have violated sacred attorney-client privilege in order to defame Charlie Dingleman. "The other day," Schmalz said, "he asked me if you, in the strict legal sense of the word, might be guilty of slander," and Judith felt her heart skip. "I assured him that rumors about Charlie were rife, and I thought that you couldn't be blamed for anything." He had managed to make her sleepless with his casual, baleful words, and these worries made it harder to put off Alfred Schmalz when he stood beside her, promising sanctuary in his large, sunless house with its walls covered by pictures of his dead wife.

Now that Judith was a partner, Alfred Schmalz let her know that the firm was not making quite so much as it had in years past, perhaps because it employed too many Democrats in a Republican age. Others repeated this theory aloud, and once Judith heard someone wishing that Charlie Dingleman were back, describing the former congressman as a jovial sort who knew lots of useful people. Judith couldn't believe that anyone would want Charlie back, but she could see that it made sense, in the summer of 1988, when Dukakis's victory was not absolutely certain, to hire someone from the Reagan administration.

The newest member of the firm was Huntington Draeb, who had just finished "quite a tour," as he put it, on the Latin American desk at State. Hunt, as he liked to be called, was in his early forties. He had a nose that was narrow like a rudder, tweezer-thin eyebrows, and spongy lips that seemed to inflate when he spoke. Within days after being introduced by an ardent Pete Thingeld, he moved into Charlie's old office and covered its walls with photographs of himself alongside famed Republicans, as well as one in which, lips stretched between grin and wonderment, he held up a Spanish-language newspaper with a headline that, translated roughly, read, "Thirty Guerrillas Killed in Firefight." With his eyes sad and moist, Alfred Schmalz told Judith, "Hunt is not a nice man, but he will be extremely good for the firm."

Draeb worked hard to ingratiate himself with the partners, and soon he invited the newest partner to lunch at his club, the mysteriously misspelled Sturling Club, which also happened to be Alfred Schmalz's club and had only recently admitted women. The club was in a rambling stone building on Massachusetts Avenue, and just behind it was a cemetery that Judith had always wondered about.

"I've been a member for three years," Huntington Draeb told her, his voice smooth with the belief that he was charming. "It meant a lot to me to be asked to join. What it said to me was my work for my country wasn't in vain."

Inside a hot cab piloted by a Sikh who seemed to be watching them in his rearview mirror, Judith felt Hunt's breath, for he sat a little too close. "Hey, chief, how about some A.C.?" Hunt asked. When the driver replied, shaking his head, that the air conditioning wasn't working, Hunt replied swiftly. Leaning across the front seat, he said, "If I find out you're lying—and believe me, I'll find out—you'll never drive in this town again, you little prick." It was less than a mile to the Sturling Club, but Hunt made Judith jittery, the way he took charge, the way he kept telling the man to shift lanes, almost yanking her from the cab when they got there. When the driver said the fare was six dollars, Hunt gave him a five-dollar bill and told him to fix his air conditioner.

. . .

HUNT GRIPPED Judith's elbow as they stepped through an entry parlor that was modeled on a seedy London ancestor; after passing cracked leather chairs, tall brass ashtrays, and portraits of dogs, they entered an equally shabby, half-empty dining room. At their table (the dark green tablecloth stained by old wine), one of the waiters, all of whom wore white gloves, appeared swiftly and just as swiftly brought their food. Judith struggled to eat her lukewarm soup and wilted Caesar salad as Hunt gobbled a plate of shrimp, a lamb chop, a pile of succotash, and several rolls covered with poppy seeds.

"I've made enemies," Hunt said, sipping cappuccino with his meal, a ring of foamed milk around his thick lips, a poppy seed stuck to a front tooth. "I've had to order the deaths of dozens, maybe hundreds, of very bad people who would have stopped at nothing to hurt the cause of freedom."

Judith nodded, as she'd been nodding throughout the meal, looking around. The waiters, all of whom seemed to know Mister Draeb, were a constant presence, pouring ice water and fetching rolls, as Hunt told Judith about his divorce ("Sheila was a wonderful woman but we never had time for each other"), about his three no-longer-small children (Kevin, Alex, and Elizabeth) whom he never saw but wished to God he had (his face drooped, then sprang back, showing the resilience of the human spirit), and about how truly excited he was, after serving nearly eight years with the administration, to be working with Thingeld, Pine. Every so often a club member would stop at their table and Judith would vaguely recognize a name or face, knowing that one had worked with Kissinger, another with Bundy or Rostow or McNamara. None looked like anyone she actually knew but rather like representatives of a tribe from a place where the custom required strong deodorant, regular applications of talcum powder, bold-striped suits, and unblinking eyes. Judith found herself shivering, but not so anyone would notice. Her skin simply tingled. When she saw Alfred Schmalz's sorrowful expression across the dining room, Hunt began to evaluate the firm, shaking his head as he offered his assessments.

"Pete Thingeld: a good guy, but a little out of it, I'd say," Hunt said. "Al Schmalz," he lowered his voice to a whisper, having seen him, "another good guy, but I can't figure out what he does anymore. I know you're very close to him." He stopped as he chewed another piece off the end of a roll. "Though I have to say, I respect him. He worked with Rusk; he knows what it's like to make life-and-death decisions. He ever talk to you about that?"

Judith shook her head, the skin on her back atingle as she thought about her private talks with Alfred Schmalz.

"Only in passing," she said.

"A lot of these people are legends," Draeb went on, pointing to his cup and waving for another cappuccino. "We come from different sides of the fence, but I have a lot of respect for a guy like Al Schmalz. We're like a club, people like us; Al, as you probably know, is a Sturling guy from way back. There wasn't a lot of margin for error in our work for Uncle. If we fucked up, people died, and sometimes we just had to hope for the best." He sipped the last of his second cappuccino. "We had to learn to live with that and try to get a good night's sleep."

A triangular crease formed just above his rudderlike nose as he spoke to Judith, breaking off only to order strawberry shortcake, but not for Judith.

"I can see you marrying a guy like Al Schmalz, like I hear you might," he said suddenly, as if that had been the subject of their conversation. "He'd give you security, a kind of status, a very comfortable life. You'd have to give him a blow job every week or so, but he wouldn't expect much more at his age, and then he'd die and you'd make sure the will was solid. What the hell?"

Judith stood, her palms pressed against the table, wanting more than anything to smack her luncheon partner. This man was far worse than anything she had even imagined about Charlie Dingleman, but she also understood that this man, unlike Charlie Dingleman, could never be hurt by someone like her.

"Why are we having lunch, Mr. Draeb?" she asked. "Why are you trying to provoke me?"

He shook his head. The strawberry shortcake was set down, red juice oozing from the sides of pale brown moist pastry, and he plunged a fork into the top.

"Sit down, sit down," he said, shrugging and filling his mouth with dessert. "I just gave you my two cents." He smiled. "Don't be offended. My language is a little rough, but I like to treat women as equals." He paused. "Hey, I'm sorry, really. I just remembered: the word around the office is that you get very easily offended."

Judith's face grew warm despite the coolness of the dining room. She looked around and nodded toward Alfred Schmalz, who she saw was sitting with the author of *My Four Trouble Spots*. Alfred's purple lower lip moved as if he would call out, but then he didn't; the memoirist turned and smiled like someone used to being recognized. As Huntington Draeb once more beckoned her to sit, she thought that she liked his sentiment about equality and did not entirely hate his smooth conceits.

"I just get offended by that kind of language," Judith said.

"Then I apologize," he said, and bowed his head to demonstrate his sorrow. Then he took a spoon and filled it with the remains of his shortcake.

Judith stared at the top of his narrow nose and saw that his spiky black hair was thinning on top and that a crooked scar ran along his scalp. She thought that she might be feeling a shoeless foot under the table and to her surprise did not mind the warmth that was now replacing her earlier tingles.

"What I don't understand," Judith said with a twitch of a smile, "is how you could consider voting for someone like Reagan or Bush.

You talk about treating women as equals, but then you support people who don't want us to have the right to choose on behalf of our own bodies." She completed her smile. "Bush is such a weenie," she finished.

Hunt smiled back, knowing, as Judith knew, that she did not really hold this against him. He was after all a Republican, and that was how they voted.

"I don't understand how you could vote for someone like Mondale," he said. "Or this guy Dukakis. Or any of them. I'm sure they're all good Americans, but I'm not sure they have the guts to defend our freedoms and our values. Simple as that."

Judith felt his five toes wiggling as his foot rubbed her calf and decided that this was amusing as long as the foot stayed below her knee. As she looked at him, she realized that his eyes said nothing about the person within whose skull they lodged. A moment later, as the under-the-table connection continued, Hunt turned to greet a man with a gray beard and wide black eyebrows; a former top person in the National Security Agency, Hunt told her when he'd left, a Sturling guy since LBJ's day.

· · ·

AFTER HUNT SIGNED for the lunch, Alfred Schmalz approached their table. "Getting acquainted?" he said, looking worriedly from Judith to Draeb, then back again, as Draeb's foot attempted to make its way under her skirt. Schmalz looked closely at Judith, who suddenly got out of her chair and smoothed her skirt.

"Hunt's given me an interesting lunch," she said, pleased to see Alfred Schmalz's eyes film with jealousy.

On the way out Judith took Draeb's arm. As they walked along the purple-and-green carpets of the entry hall and into the bright early-summer heat, Judith saw that some of the men in the leather chairs were watching them. "Come back soon," the NSA man with the gray beard and large black eyebrows said. Sitting in a corner was

Robert McNamara, his hair stringy white, his face covered with spots, a stipple of foam at the corner of his mouth. Judith nodded to him, not at first recognizing him but sensing that she somehow knew him, and just as she realized who he was, McNamara politely nodded back.

TWENTY-SEVEN

Hank Morriday liked to imagine himself in a Mussolini-sized office, one with a long sofa, which led his thoughts to the dark-haired woman who was probably named Robin. He could see her stopping by his new quarters, wearing her blue sleeveless dress, then slipping off her stockings; he could hear the snap of her dark blue brassiere. Then, knowing what came next, Hank locked the door of his modest office, reached for a tissue, and brought this fantasy to its private, embarrassed conclusion.

When Hank stepped out to dispose of his tissue, a pair of senior Fellows approached him in the corridor, chatting about an upcoming lunch to which he wasn't invited, and they were followed by the Institute's director, Randolph Maintree, who put out his hand in greeting, which forced Hank to shift the tissue to his left hand before reciprocating. After he returned to his office he carefully arranged the few books on his desk; still not satisfied, he opened one and marked two paragraphs with yellow highlighter. He'd meant to borrow more from the Institute's library, the better to add weight to his shelves, and thought perhaps that he'd get around to that today. Then he closed his eyes and, as he thought about people loosing the bonds of welfare dependency, took a short nap.

Hank was unusually jumpy and supposed that had something to do with Dukakis's imminent nomination. His edginess only got worse when he saw how far Dukakis had gone ahead in the polls, even in Texas. Hank had come to dread the morning newspapers, and as he ate breakfast in the warm mustiness of his apartment (a mousy scurrying came from the walls), he would stroke his beard and sip the astringent cup of Nescafé that he'd prepared with a soup spoon and feel further behind.

Hank had also been a little jumpy because Candy Romulade was so aflutter. He had never seen her this chattily distracted, but she couldn't stop complaining about a fund-raising event for Dukakis that Big Tooth had helped to plan, and she didn't seem to notice Hank's keen interest whenever she mentioned the "bimbo television star" who was supposed to show up.

. . .

CANDY WAS PARTICULARLY SNAPPISH by the time the night arrived, and Hank worried about her temper from the moment he stepped into the extravagant hotel lobby, surrounded at once by men in tuxedos and women with bare shoulders and wobbly heels. As Hank followed the stream of people up escalators and into the Centennial Room, which had lustrous gold-and-blue wallpaper and chandeliers as big as refrigerators, he was prepared to give this night his highest rating.

Candy had been in the hotel all day, seeing to everything (That poster isn't straight! We need more chairs!), then had rushed to the Big Tooth hospitality suite to change, furious that her dark green ball gown did not quite fit but more furious at feeling like an errand boy, hating her job—her "fucking job," she kept muttering. As soon as he pushed through the deep, sober crowd that surrounded the only bartender, Hank saw Candy pacing the periphery; he saw that a faint band of heat rash made a bridge between her collarbones.

"Have you seen Teresa?" she asked, as a dour electric band on a faraway platform played "Coming to America" and "Happy Days Are Here Again." Hank's cummerbund kept slipping; his pretied bow tie kept tilting. He always had these problems when he dressed up, and once more he realized that a penumbra of unkemptness accompanied him. But he would not want to be anywhere else, he thought as he looked around the Centennial Room, where suddenly the brightness of camera lights made him squint.

It was at that moment, when those lights flared white and the crowd stirred, that Hank knew she was there. Just that knowledge was enough to make him rise up on his toes, stretching his neck, although all he could see at first was the black-and-white clothing of people dressed like him or the pinched skin of women dressed like Candy. But when he saw those waves of auburn hair, his heart raced, as if he had run many miles to reach this point in life.

"*Now* what?" Candy said, lighting a cigarette, inhaling so that her cheeks caved in. Under her breath she added, "Dukakis isn't at the airport yet, and he'd better show. Who's running that fucking campaign?" Under another breath she asked, "Where's Teresa?"

Hank smiled gently. How was he to tell Candy that he'd just gotten his first glimpse of Wendy Lullabay, his favorite actress in all the world, the woman who appeared on *Perfect Fit*, his favorite television program in all the world?

"It's that Hollywood person who's supposed to be here, I think," Hank said indifferently, lifting himself on his toes again, his eyes fastened on that auburn hair; and then, beneath the clutter of cables and onlookers, Hank saw her legs, tanned, rising from purple shoes with very high heels.

Candy shook her head. "That bimbo is not what people are paying five hundred for," she said. "Heads will roll if Mike doesn't show up soon. My head," she added with an ironic smile. "Why do I get stuck with this shit?"

Hank was barely listening, so eager was he to get another glimpse of Wendy Lullabay. (What color was her dress?) Uncharitably he wished that Candy would stop her yammering. In his mind he had by now left the Centennial Room and was watching the opening credits of *Perfect Fit*. There Wendy Lullabay tried on clothes and finally frolicked, her large, very natural breasts abob in an azure bathing suit, sand between her lovely toes, her legs frozen in taut perfection as she leaped toward the net and smacked a volleyball, the cleft of her buttocks suddenly, alarmingly, filling the screen as the image faded away. Hank almost told Candy to shut up, for she was still complaining; because he'd had to bend to hear another of her whines, he'd lost track of the actress: the lights, the auburn hair, the purple shoes were out of sight. Had she perhaps gone to "freshen up"?

"You seem really fidgety," Candy said, looking at her watch, which now showed nine o'clock. "You know, you could do me a big favor. You could go to the suite and try to find out where the Dukakis party is right now; let me know exactly when they're on the ground."

Hank looked at her in shock. For all he knew his favorite actress was about to go back to L.A., as who wouldn't, given the choice between leaping on a sandy beach and standing in this crowd in a place like Washington. Nearby Hank saw a senator—he recognized first his silvery hair, more polished than combed—talking to a woman he'd seen before, the probable Robin (this time wearing a red dress), she managing to let her chest graze the senator's hand, which clutched a tall glass of golden bubbles. The senator nodded to Hank, a recognition that he'd been recognized, and Hank nodded back, murmuring, "Good to see ya," as if they were old pals. Robin stared at Hank, almost as if she knew how she'd participated in his recent fantasy. Where on earth had Wendy Lullabay gone?

"It would be a big help to me," Candy Romulade was saying, a little louder because the band was louder, "but you don't seem to be listening to a word I'm saying. Is something wrong?"

Hank shook his head. Nothing was wrong except that Candy was continuing to talk. Who gave a flying fuck about Dukakis, that Greek dwarf? And there she was!

Because he had briefly lost sight of the actress, Hank was not pre-pared to see her at such close range, life-sized in a short turquoise dress. No more than twenty feet away, she was shaking hands with the silvery senator, her startlingly wide smile so close that for a mo-ment Hank could not manage a complete breath. Hank could see hints of blue at the tops of Wendy Lullabay's breasts, nearly ex-posed, and follicles along her perfect legs and a slightly darker color at the roots of her auburn hair, and he inspected her as if she were from another galaxy, which in a way she was.

"I can't believe it, that woman coming here dressed like that," Candy said under her breath, and lighted another cigarette, sucking on it until a uniformed hotel employee told her that she was break-ing the law. Smoke came out of her mouth and nose for nearly thirty seconds.

Hank could not unfasten his eyes and began to feel the angry weight of jealousy as he watched Wendy Lullabay and the senator, now only inches apart. A large circle surrounded them.

"I guess you're so enamored," Candy was saying to Hank, "that I'll have to go to the suite. You know, I really don't appreciate this, when I take you to something, not to help." She shook her head, looking again at her watch, not quite believing Hank's trance. "This is horrible," she said. "We're fucked. I'm fucked."

Candy spoke that way only when she was most wound up, and Hank backed away as if to avoid the contagion. He felt immobilized. On his left was this tense woman whom he'd been seeing and had become quite fond of; on his right was a woman he did not know but with whom he'd been close in another, more private way. Whenever she moved, her dress lifted above her interesting knees; she had a mesmerizing bosom that swelled and moved during those gestures, coming closer each time to revealing its final colors. At that moment Hank believed that if he never had to move from this spot, surrounded by people he did not know and listening to a de-

pressed band playing "California, Here I Come," he would somehow be content.

The Centennial Room had meanwhile become packed. Hank
saw Candy smiling for the first time, and then she dashed away,
muttering, "Jesus, it's about time!" It was evident that the presump-
tive nominee had arrived, and moments later Hank got a glimpse of
a short man with stiff dark hair. Wendy Lullabay stretched to view
the arrival and Hank couldn't take his eyes from the stretch.

"He's a dear, dear man," Hank heard the actress say to the senator, the first time he'd heard her voice as it actually emerged from
her lips, as it did on television. He moved closer so as not to miss a
word but also so as not to miss the chance to commit every pore to
memory.

"It's our first real chance at welfare reform in eight years," Hank
said, and he found it peculiar to hear a voice that was his own and
which had all at once sprung from his mouth. The senator looked at
Hank as if he were an intruder, despite their earlier hearty greeting,
so Hank gave up on him and directed his words to Wendy Lullabay.
"The governor could fix a very leaky system," Hank told her, speaking a little more slowly because he knew the actress might not be familiar with his views on the subject. "He has the tools to do it, and
he knows what needs to be fixed."

Before Wendy Lullabay could respond, the senator did a very
rude thing. He turned his back on Hank and by doing so, blocked
Hank's view of the actress. Only a tawny arm with gold down could
be spotted, then that magical chest, then her large, though not entirely focused, hazel eyes, but no longer at the same time. Fury
overtook Hank; he could have strangled that dickhead senator.

It was in the midst of these heated thoughts that Hank was
pushed aside by arriving guests: the Secret Service; the Massachusetts governor himself, dark suit and white shirt; Candy Romulade,
her face contorted by tension; and other, almost familiar faces, all of

them keeping the pace until the nominee was face-to-face with the senator and the actress. Flashbulbs scattered more fresh light, and as the Massachusetts governor and the California actress shook hands, Hank saw the friendly grin and oddly baffled eyes of Reynolds Mund, the local anchorman, and at his side was Candy's assistant, looking dazed and a little worried; far back he thought he saw Judith Grust and the old guy she was supposed to marry and next to them a diminished Robin. As the band replayed "Happy Days Are Here Again," Wendy Lullabay began to dance, arms above her head, hands clapping. Hank clapped with her, but no one else joined this exercise, and he saw Candy's disapproving gaze. She was watching him as if he had lost his mind and Hank realized that, for just a moment, he had. A moment later he leveled his bow tie, which had gone vertical.

When Dukakis moved into the crowd, Hank thought it would be all right to continue his conversation with the actress, who had been listening to the senator. He casually put out his hand and said, "Hank Morriday," leaving his limb extended. "Someday, if you're interested, I would love to explain more about coordinating welfare payments with individual initiative." Hank looked around. "Mike understands that, you can bet on it."

When finally Wendy Lullabay took his hand in greeting, Hank was surprised by the coolness, the delicacy of her fingers. He stared into her green-brown eyes and said softly, "I never miss your show, never."

She was pulling, he realized, her hand away, and someone nearby, who turned out to be Crane, his doppelganger, was giggling, although everyone else seemed to be watching the Massachusetts governor, who had gone speedily to the bandstand from where he was to give a speech about good jobs for good wages. The crowd shifted again, and Hank felt his upper arm gripped tight by one of the men who'd arrived with the governor, a silent fellow with a tiny mustache and an earplug, and when Hank looked back, all he could see was a wave of auburn hair and tawny ankles and purple high-heeled shoes and the tips of her fingers as she brushed the cheek of the senator with silvery hair, fingers he had just managed, briefly, briefly, to touch with his own.

TWENTY-EIGHT

As the summer wore on, Charlie Dingleman noticed that Reynolds Mund, who once had been his favorite local anchorman, appeared to have something growing on his nose. Mund was otherwise acting strangely—the way that he now and then mumbled something that sounded like "losing news about schools" or "truly mollifying fools" or some such. Charlie supposed that he himself had been acting strangely too, including one forty-eight-hour stretch when he more or less retreated to his bed, letting the light of the television fill the room with the haze of apprehension. He had to admit that there had been an odd pleasure in pitying himself, in splashing around his pond of private misery; he had even neglected *My Four Trouble Spots*, setting it aside after a chapter entitled "Ruminations," in which the memoirist wrote:

> When we diplomats touch down on foreign shores, the hand we extend does not make political distinctions. It is, in point of fact, neither a Republican hand nor a Democratic hand. Indeed, because I speak bluntly, I often tell my foreign hosts that the hand with which I wipe myself is not my ambassadorial hand. They hesitantly take my fingers of friendship even if they don't instantly grasp my more subtle point. My wife has often warned me to soften my salty tongue, but I long ago learned the value of direct speech, for it was instilled in me

during my year at Oxford. My forthright hand, I'm told, is firm but honest.

It was my right hand that I extended to the president at the conclusion of my last assignment. We had of course known one another for years, and he had always been most grateful for my personal generosity to his war chest. This time our meeting was short and cordial. He asked me how I wanted to serve our country and shook his head sadly when I told him how eager I was to continue my mission in the Foreign Service.

"We can't send you out there again," he said, refusing, I thought, to make eye contact. "You've earned a rest—a long one."

"Mr. President," I began. But as I pled my case, I could see that the press of urgent business had distracted him. His brow furrowed, and I was struck by how high office had aged him. We parted with mutual respect and, I believe, the sort of closeness that comes only to men who understand what it means to work toward a common goal.

Charlie's own ruminations tended to be about another, make-believe life, one in which he had won reelection and remained with Abigail. In this life he would have a sauna in the House gym or a tennis game with his pal Fred Hykler; on a warm Sunday morning he'd mow the lawn while Abigail, her hair damp with exertion, pulled up weeds. Charlie had been thinking a lot about Abigail since she'd called to scold him about missing Jessica's graduation; it was as if Eve had never existed, apart from those few possessions she'd left behind. He sometimes thought about Abigail with that James fellow: in bed—*their* bed—on Sunday morning, with James touching her in some familiar way, stroking her hair, her freckled legs, as Charlie once had. He couldn't watch! He

wondered what James looked like and if they actually slept together and if so, how often and in what style. He wondered if
James would answer the telephone if he called.

A few days later Charlie drank a Scotch and a few minutes later
called Abigail to ask if maybe they could meet, perhaps for a drink,
as he was sure they had talked about doing.

"What about your little office companion and wife?" she asked.

Charlie shook his head. "Eve is history," he said.

"What a pity," Abigail replied.

Charlie thought that she sounded sympathetic.

"Could James come too?" she asked.

"I wouldn't want that," he replied, and after nearly a full minute
of silence, he added, "You're not serious."

Abigail didn't say anything, and Charlie tried to persuade himself
that she was flirting or trying to make him jealous. "Charlie," she
said, "the problem is that I really, truly hate the life that you seem to
miss so much."

"What life?" he replied.

"I'm actually very happy now," she added, and Charlie was almost
positive that he'd misunderstood what she'd just said.

. . .

As it happened, it was on a Sunday in August of 1988 that Charlie's own separate life began to take shape, although he did not yet
know it. All he knew was that by the time it was almost dark and he
was still not dressed, he was thinking about how to right himself.
Wearing khakis and a T-shirt ("Tufts, Class of '88") that did not flat-
ter him, he went for a walk and soon regretted it. The streets of
Georgetown were empty, the shops were closed, and the darkness of
the alphabet streets was alarming. He stopped at a restaurant on
Wisconsin Avenue, attracted by the sight of sentient humans, but
when he stepped inside and sat at the long bar, he didn't want to
drink; above all he didn't want to pay four dollars and fifty cents for

a bottle of beer. He glanced at his puffy face and mussed hair in the mirror behind the bottle display and momentarily met the eyes of a woman of uncertain age, who turned away just as Charlie did. Charlie looked to his right and nodded; the woman's short legs were crossed and she rocked on her bar stool.

"Hey," Charlie said.

"Hey," she replied.

"Hot night," he said.

"Why aren't we at the beach?" she replied. "Are we crazy?"

Charlie sipped his expensive beer. The mere act of conversation and the sight of those short legs, now crossed the other way, aroused him. Who knew? He moved down a stool and saw that the woman was younger than he'd supposed. She looked away, then turned and pointed at his T-shirt.

"Did you just graduate?" she asked.

Charlie, who was not about to admit having a college-aged daughter, said, "A friend gave it to me." Her crossed legs glowed, and he looked at his beer. He moved again so that one bar stool separated them.

"Actually, I know who you are," she said.

"Oh, my," Charlie replied with a helpless smile. "How come?"

"I interned on the Hill when you were there," she said, and added, "I'm really sorry you lost."

"Me too," Charlie said, and he peered at her, as if to recall her better. But he had no idea who she was.

"So what are you doing now? You don't look very happy. I hope you don't mind my saying that."

"Good question," Charlie replied, although he had no intention of answering.

"I really, really want to go back to the Hill," she said. "I loved it. I learned so much. Do you know anyone there? Maybe this is just the luckiest thing for me—I mean that you walked in."

Charlie moved one more stool over. He gulped down the rest of his beer and felt a little woozy. He looked down at her hand, contemplating the capture of five warm fingers, and it was in the midst of these transports that she smiled in a way he could not interpret.

"I know a few people," he said, and added, "You're very pretty."

When she didn't respond, Charlie tried to think of something funny; the next time he turned, she was gone, which left him alone at a bar on a Sunday night in August. Was it something he'd said? The dim light outside promised coolness, but the heat and moisture in the air was intense, and as he returned to the deserted streets of Georgetown, he began sweating horribly; he even felt a little short of breath and wondered about his heart and lungs. It did not help his mood to know that his neighbors were in better places, settling down inside weathered beach houses in Nantucket and the Vineyard or planning victory for the brand-new nominees, Bush and Dukakis. Charlie blinked, but an afterimage of short, bare legs remained.

When he got back to his house, he discovered two unpleasant things: he had either lost or forgotten his keys, and he very much needed to use the bathroom. In fact he was so looking forward to this that he stood in almost painful anticipation as he reached for the key that wasn't, at that moment, there. "Oh, shit," he said, and then repeated the phrase.

He marched about his tiny yard and kicked the dirt, looking there and on the sidewalk for a shiny object that might be his key, which shared a chain with the key to his 1986 Oldsmobile Cutlass and the key to the house in McLean, which he couldn't let go of. He knew he wouldn't find it—now he was sure it was in another pair of trousers—but giving up meant facing unwanted decisions: how to get in and what to do about the immediate problem.

Charlie finally decided to use one of the rhododendrons in front of the house, but as he squirmed and squatted, he saw that an upstairs light in the house to the left was on and so was a downstairs light in the house to the right. Charlie crouched lower, faced his own house, and unzipped, finding that it was an awkward position from which to perform that feat and that there were unwanted side effects. But he knew that his pants would dry and his shoes could be polished, and now at least he could walk back to Wisconsin Avenue and call a locksmith. He was having these thoughts when he saw the red and white lights of a police cruiser, which stopped right in front of his house. Seconds later a spotlight shined into his face.

"Oh, shit," Charlie said again.

"Please stay where you are," said an amplified voice as one of the policemen, a black man with large hands, got out of the cruiser. Charlie's heart fluttered. "And please raise your hands," the man, whose name was Officer Louis and who was watching Charlie closely, added.

"Anything wrong?" Charlie asked, as Officer Louis was joined by an older white man with a tiny mouth like a bottle cap.

"We're trying to find that out, sir," the white policeman, Officer Quella, said as Charlie's heart slowed. "We had a complaint."

"A complaint?" Charlie asked.

"About a prowler—someone lurking and maybe exposing himself," Quella said, his wee lips pronouncing each word slowly.

"You look like you've had an accident, sir," Officer Louis said, his eyes on Charlie's fly, which was open.

"What are you talking about? This is my house," Charlie said.

"Why aren't you inside it on this hot-as-hell night?" Quella asked.

"If it were me, sir, I would be inside with the air conditioning, maybe watching a ball game, not walking around my front yard with my dick hanging out," Louis said.

Charlie looked down but did not respond to Officer Louis's exaggeration.

"Do you have some identification?" Quella asked.

"It's in the house, with my keys," Charlie said, feeling an impulse to run as the two policemen stared at him and seemed, he thought, to be reaching for their service revolvers. "My house," he added.

"We'd appreciate it, sir, if you'd sit with us in the cruiser while we fill out a report," Officer Louis said. Charlie noticed that faces peered from the windows of several houses, no doubt wild with curiosity, and he thought that at least one of those faces belonged to a low-down informant. He tried again to explain, but the two policemen regarded him as if he were a child—not dismissing his story entirely, but not gullible either. By the time he sat on the hot vinyl backseat of their Ford sedan, while red and white lights blinked overhead, he was no longer aware of the dampness in his clothes.

TWENTY-NINE

In THE SUMMER OF 1988 Martin Himmelschaft was not paying attention to the news, not even when Reynolds Mund talked about the fires in Yellowstone Park or when the weatherman with the long pointer joked about Imelda Marcos's shoes, which seemed to annoy the anchorman. What Martin did watch were those moments when someone would reveal an occurrence so hideous, so unnerving, that viewers all around the city would shake their heads and murmur, "Awful!" and when the anchorman's nose would twitch as he muttered something unintelligible. More often, the anchorman was saying unintelligible things—Martin almost thought he heard "molecules." It happened again after a report about a triple murder in Prince George's County, a crime (Mund blinked, giving his trademark downcast look) that "startled even police by its sheer brutality," a favorite Mundian phrase.

One late-August day a red-and-blue envelope arrived addressed to Mr. Martin Himmelschaft and Ms. Teresa Maracopulos, and when Martin, who got home first, examined it, he saw that they'd been invited to a celebration of Reynolds Mund's twentieth anniversary as an anchorman. But this, like so much else these days, was unwelcome; he saw the words "Black Tie" in a lower corner of the invitation as a threat. He'd rather play poker with his pals, and he missed that old life. Martin wished that just once Teresa would come along to Baltimore with the O's Folks or even watch a game with him on television, although it would be late tonight: the Orioles were playing on the West Coast. He loved Eddie Murray.

Martin knew that he shouldn't let every little thing affect him so. But this summer everything did, and part of it was because he was almost certain that his dear, dear wife was seeing someone else, probably screwing him. More than once he'd woken up and found their bed empty; each time he'd found Teresa on the downstairs sofa in the dark, staring at nothing, as if in a trance. The one time he had hinted at the forbidden subject, she had wrapped her arms around her legs, all bent over, and said, "Martin, I don't ever want to lie to you, but it's something I just can't talk about." When Martin examined the invitation to that fancy party, he was tempted to tear it up, but of course Teresa would know; she was probably helping to give the party. He thought about leaving her, yet he loved her so.

. . .

ONE MORNING SOON AFTER, Martin sat in his cream-and-brown downtown office and tried to listen when other people spoke to him, when Ginny Lou, one cubicle away, gaily asked, "How's it going, baby?" and LaScala, the pretty nineteen-year-old who'd just come to work in personnel, nagged him about some statistical reports, "Because if you don't do those reports, Mr. Himmelschaft, then there's nobody who can do their job around here, if you get what I'm saying." Martin got what she was saying, but he'd been thinking about something he'd overheard Teresa saying on the telephone, something about a lunch at Barkley's, and there was something about her lowered voice that had made Martin strain to hear every syllable.

A little past noon, then, on that August day, Martin Himmelschaft took the Metro to a downtown very different from the one he'd known in 1955, and as he did so he remembered what it had been like to travel around Washington by streetcar, before the fires. He hadn't yet decided actually to visit Barkley's, and as he rode the escalator from the subway tunnel into the early afternoon heat, as he was bumped by hurrying men and women in dark suits, he felt almost lost; when a pack of black limousines sped by, led by motorcycles and police cars, sirens shrilling, windows smoky, Martin imagined that Reagan himself must be inside one of them. He passed a young beggar with a blond goatee and looked down at his unfriendly face. A half-eaten banana, quickly turning black, lay in a corner of his gray wool blanket, as did a small pocketknife and a leather-bound volume of poetry by Longfellow. From a front pocket Martin retrieved all of his coins, which came to eighteen cents, and dropped them swiftly into an upturned hat. "Don't break yourself, man," the beggar said, as the pack of limousines returned, accompanied by its phalanx of motorcycle cops. Several cars carried the five-colored flag of an unknown nation, and Martin stopped to watch the noisy procession with its bragging sirens.

Martin realized that he couldn't help himself, that he'd walked the two blocks to Barkley's because otherwise he would have gotten nothing done at work, never finished those reports. He stood in the sunny street and regarded the restaurant's inner darkness as an alien universe. Although he hadn't meant to, he then went inside and peered into the dark, connected rooms, noticing that all of them were crammed with lunch eaters straining to hear one another. He soon found himself part of a small crowd waiting for tables, behind a family from Nebraska who'd heard about Barkley's and were staring at the uniform worn by Walter Johnson, that remarkable man who won 414 games for the Senators. These tourists had hoped to see a famous personage but recognized almost no one in this noisy place.

Martin looked around just like the Nebraskans, seeing a few local celebrities that these out-of-towners would not know. They would not, for instance, have recognized Suzanne Smule, several tables away, although she had made five network appearances in the last two weeks to talk about the width and breadth of Gorbachev's vision, not to mention the importance of Eduard Shevardnadze. They did not realize that she was much sought after for her knowledge of perestroika and as someone who advised Michael Dukakis. One of her tablemates was Randolph Maintree, another unfamiliar face but, one could agree, a distinguished one; he had a deep tan, the result of three weeks spent on the Vineyard. Had the Nebraska family been careful readers of history, they might have come across younger versions of this man in blurry photographs of shiny conference tables surrounded by leaders and advisers. Yet neither Martin nor the Nebraskans were entirely disappointed by this grouping, for these two were about to be joined by Brandon Sladder, a chubby columnist with a petulant expression, someone that all of them were positively sure they'd seen on television talking about Dukakis and Bush, just as they'd seen the Redskin linebacker who was munching crab cakes across the room.

For Martin, as the Barkley's crowd expanded, it was as if all the men and women in gray suits were watching an event that vanished at the center. The late-August sun sent streaks of light onto these phalanges (handshakes and rapid smiles) that pressed toward the tables. Martin watched as the Nebraskan, who was an accountant and developer, kept patting the shoulder of his eleven-year-old son, who looked possessively at his shopping bag, which contained relics from the Smithsonian. He watched as a busboy spilled a basket of rolls onto the floor and as Randolph Maintree patted Suzanne Smule's heavy thigh and let his hand linger for a few inappropriate seconds while Sladder, the columnist, sat down next to them.

"We've been talking about the new Russian revolution," Suzanne Smule said to Sladder, with whom she'd often exchanged thoughts.

"As usual Suzie is giving us fascinating ideas to chew over," Maintree said, extending his dry, courteous hand before returning it to the thigh beside him. "It could turn out to be very interesting," Sladder said, and reported that he'd just come back from a briefing at the State Department. "Fascinating," Maintree said again, shaking his large head for emphasis. For several minutes the threesome meditated aloud on unresolved conflicts among the world's great and small powers.

The Nebraskans heard none of this, and Martin was not even trying to pay attention, for at that instant he spotted his wife, who was wearing a blue-and-white summer dress that showed off her slightly heavy bare legs, and she was moving toward a favored round table at the center of the main room where, Martin saw, the anchorman Reynolds Mund sat by himself and chewed up a plate of soft-shell crabs. Had the Nebraskans looked closely, they would have seen that Mund had forgotten to shave his right cheek, but their gazes did not linger there, for they did not watch the local news and therefore did not even know that he was famous. Martin watched, quite fascinated, for it *was*—there was no mistaking it—Teresa who not only headed toward the anchorman's table but sat beside him and stroked his neck and patted the cluster of hair that grew along his crooked nose. Martin could not move. It was as if Teresa were a stranger and not his own wife, especially when she chatted so excitedly and reached down and tore a stringy piece of soft-shell crab from the anchorman's helping and swallowed it.

The Nebraskans, who were being ignored by the maitre d' as if he knew they did not belong, began to look around impatiently, and soon their son complained that he was getting hungry and that he wished he were at the Hickory House back home. After a few more minutes of this, the family decided to get lunch at a Burger King they'd spotted down the street, a familial sulk that went wholly unappreciated. Martin did not know whether to stay or to go; his eyes were blinking and his hands were vibrating as he thought of rushing up to that table, the one where his own wife, lovingly it appeared, whispered something into the ear of the anchorman. Martin felt a dizzy uncertainty and knew that all he should do now was leave. By the doorway, close to the Walter Johnson uniform, he saw a large green dish that held a pile of Barkley's matchbooks, and as he reached for one he felt an uncontrollable, raging impulse; the dish was heavier than it looked, and Martin surprised everyone around him, including the Nebraskans, when he picked it up and threw it as hard as he could at a wall, shattering the photograph of Sam Rayburn.

"Sorry," he said when he realized what he'd done, and then he ran for it.

THIRTY

Charlie Dingleman never imagined that he'd have more to do with Candy Romulade, not when he risked being reminded about his Big Tooth bill, which he had every intention of paying but which was very large and ominously itemized. But neither did he think he'd be talking again to Skip Haine at the White House, who telephoned one morning and said, "I'll bet you're surprised to hear from me."

"I know you're a man of your word," Charlie replied in the jovial voice that he used to take along when he campaigned.

"Well, it *is* me, sir," Skip Haine said, "and this time I believe I've got some good news."

"I could use it," Charlie said, managing a chuckle.

"Here's the deal," Skip said. "Your name came up again over here, and no one could remember why it all went south in the first place."

"Don't ask me," Charlie said.

"We know the road got real bumpy," Skip continued, "but we took a closer look—the FBI and all that—and, long story short, traffic's moving smoothly now."

Skip Haine went on to say that they saw Charlie in an important role—short-term, but who knew?—working on issues, as Skip put it, that "affect real people." Charlie was about to ask what that meant or what would happen to him after the election, but he didn't want to raise any doubts. Skip seemed to anticipate these thoughts when he said, "Also, sir, we can't imagine anyone will want to stand in your way at this juncture in time."

For several hours someone looking at Charlie would say that he bounced as he walked; they would notice that he clapped his hands and, a little creakily, kneeled to do push-ups, managing one but determined to do more someday. When he heard a car go by playing a Marvin Gaye song at top volume, he wondered, "What's going on?" Charlie recalled every word that Skip Haine had just uttered and thought about who to tell, pacing happily about. Oh, this was great, he thought, just great—the White House!—and eventually he dialed Abigail's number, excited at the thought of telling her that he was in the game again, just like that.

"I have news," he said, and told her the news.

There was a short pause, after which Abigail laughed a little strangely and said, "That's nice for you."

"What's wrong?" Charlie asked, baffled by her inexplicable lack of enthusiasm.

"Nothing," she said. "It's very nice for you."

Charlie found himself remembering a night toward the end of his last campaign, at a middle school in the most rural part of the district. Seventeen people had showed up and sat in metal chairs in the basement cafeteria, which smelled of mashed potatoes and overcooked broccoli. After a twenty-minute talk there were a few hostile questions, two from men who accused Charlie of indifference to Pennsylvania's fish and waterways and one from a woman who asked about his divorce. "Don't you care about your wife and family?" she'd asked a little shrilly. After Charlie had said, "I do, very much," he'd turned to his aide-de-camp, Eve, as if in search of a better answer while he thought about the way her tiny panties barely covered her. That night he knew that he'd lose the election and in some way, though only for a short time, didn't care. Now he cared again.

"I want to see you," Charlie said, and he added, "You could share this with me."

"Oh, Charlie, *shit!*" she replied.

"I'll take that as maybe," he said, and was a little startled when she hung up.

. . .

A FEW DAYS LATER Charlie saw his name in boldface in the *Post*, accompanied by the phrase "short-short-term," but that, he supposed, is what led to another call: this one came from that television producer, the Nancyperson, the one who had tormented him last time, and someone, it turned out, who regularly inspected police reports from fancy neighborhoods like Georgetown.

"Of course I have no comment," Charlie told her when she said what she wanted. "I forgot my keys and locked myself out; where's the comment? Okay, maybe that's the comment."

"That's not what the police report says," the Nancyperson replied, gently and softly. "Actually, Mr. Dingleman, it is very specific about your behavior."

"Don't do anything stupid," Charlie said a little breathlessly, and after regarding the telephone receiver for a few more seconds and wishing he had phrased that more diplomatically, he hung up.

Charlie began to box, punching the air around him, several left jabs and one astounding uppercut. He believed that he had parted from those two cops on good terms; they had got him into the house (Officer Quella was skilled with a credit card), and sure enough his keys had been in a pocket of yesterday's trousers. When his telephone rang again, Charlie didn't answer. As soon as it stopped ringing, he called Candy Romulade, who did not sound like the Candy he'd known.

"Part of you must feel very good," she said. "You must also feel like dirt," she went on almost gaily, "like total shit, shunned, confused—like someone in a street brawl who doesn't know what hit him. Am I right?"

Charlie nodded; she was right, all right. It was as if she'd seen him punching the air.

"I hear you nodding," she said. "We're communicating!"

"Yes, we are," Charlie replied.

"I know you want me to do something to get you back on your feet," she said, "and I'd like nothing more. But I can't at this moment think of how."

"Right," Charlie said. "I hear you."

"It's not a good time," she added. "For me. Over here."

In the past Candy had sometimes talked without pausing for breath, and Charlie had appreciated the fevered authority of her voice, even if he never quite paid attention to the words themselves. Now she sounded almost chilly, as if he were some deadbeat; or perhaps she was depressed, he couldn't tell. He shut his eyes and thought about the creases of tension on her tanned face.

"Are you listening, Charlie?" she asked.

"I hear you," he said again. "But can we maybe use part of the last action plan? I mean, it ended up just lying there in a drawer."

Candy was silent, as if she were thinking.

"I was remembering something you once said," Charlie went on, and he hated the way he sounded—as if he were begging. "That your friend, your assistant, knows what's-his-name, that anchorman."

"They seem to be very close," Candy said. Her voice was a little raspy—the cost, she said when he asked if she had a cold, of smoking cartons of cigarettes and trying to organize a big gala for that very person.

"She could make it stop, I'll bet," Charlie said insistently, staring at the blackened ficus and at his pile of hostile mail; empty spaces marked every stage of his separation from domesticity. "The bell hasn't rung yet."

"Look, I'll try," Candy said finally, after a pause, almost as if she were talking to herself.

THIRTY-ONE

As the vile moist haze of a Washington summer reached its peak, Hank Morriday discovered that he'd begun to savor Michael Dukakis's decline, especially when he thought about the people who had conjoined their fates to the Massachusetts governor's. He tried to keep this gleeful emotion to himself, but whenever a new poll came out, each one showing a sinking Dukakis vessel, he found himself nodding with pleasure, trying to imagine the disappointment that would be felt by Crane and Suzanne Smule and the rest of them.

One Monday in early September Hank arrived at the Institute and found an anonymous note lodged in his mail slot. "GOOFBALL!" it said. He then wrote a note of his own: "ASSHOLE!" was its conjecture, and he placed it in the cubbyhole that belonged to Crane, an exchange of messages that could be traced, Hank thought, to a moment several days earlier at a nearby Peoples drugstore. Hank had been in a slow checkout line carrying toothpaste and a bottle of shampoo; he had also been trying not to smell an unusually strong deodorant from an unknown source when after a while he noticed that the source was the person in front of him—Crane, who was trying to hide whatever it was he was carrying.

"Hi," Hank said when acknowledgment was unavoidable.

Crane looked over his shoulder. "Yeah," he replied, and then stared ahead, making more of an effort to conceal his purchase, a vitamin supplement.

"Line never moves," Hank said, and Crane then made a dash to the right, where a second register was opening. Hank pursued him. "What's that stuff you're carrying?" Hank asked, a little breathless, bending his neck slightly to see the label on the bottle. "You got some kind of deficiency?"

"Fuck you," Crane said as he stepped to the counter, where he apologized several times to a chubby woman with a ponytail, who inspected his purchase. "I was talking to *him*," Crane insisted, but Hank pretended not to know Crane. "You're a mess," Crane said, turning so that only Hank, who quickly checked his fly, could hear him.

· · ·

HANK DID NOT THINK that he was a mess. Nevertheless, embarrassment often occupies the spotlight of one's memory; when his guard was down, usually in the hour or so before dawn, he'd recall his encounter with Wendy Lullabay and his speedy leave-taking onto a hot summer street filled by police cars and stretch limousines and spectators. Hank knew that he had done nothing untoward—he'd clapped his hands, made a solid point about welfare, and danced a wee bit—but after that evening he noticed that a distinct stillness seemed to follow him about. Whenever he ran into the Institute's director, Randolph Maintree would try to get away, although they did chat about the weather or the progress of some baffling construction work next to a second-floor urinal. Hank once attempted to discuss the football season, which he botched by not knowing the name of the Redskins' coach. At that point the director removed a wide-bowled pipe from the breast pocket of his summer jacket and placed its stem between his lips, sucking it briskly, producing a rattle of moist air. "If you have a problem," he said then, looking at the ceiling, a burbling sound emerging from the unlit pipe, "we have a first-rate counseling program."

Hank nodded in gratitude and only later realized that the director hadn't said a word about his welfare work in progress, a signal that the headmaster had become incurious about the student's future.

A day later Hank ran into Suzanne Smule next to the elevator in the chilly marble lobby. She was carrying a monograph about Kazakhstan and told Hank how sorry she was that they couldn't include him at the Dukakis lunch. His heart stopped for the instant it took him to realize that his absence from the lunch, which he'd known nothing about, was no mere ticket shortage.

"I'll be away anyway," he said.

"That's too bad," she said, with what sounded to Hank like feral insincerity.

"Yeah, well, it *is* too bad," he said. Then he added, with some spirit, "The guy's a goner anyway. He's beyond help; he's down the toilet."

Any lingering trace of interest drained from Suzanne Smule's face.

"So you'd better pack up all your own good advice for another four years," Hank went on, almost gaily, for some reason shifting into rural dialect. "Cause this guy's not gonna move off the shelf. You can shovel on the manure, but he's just not gonna grow."

Something about Suzanne Smule always aroused Hank, and it did so now as he sniffed, enjoying a new scent, something like burnt peach.

"It's Bush, Bush, Bush!" he called after her, but she didn't turn, although a young intern heard his words and gave Hank a worried look. Looking back on it, Hank supposed it might have been that moment when he first considered writing a piece to announce to the world that he would support George Bush.

. . .

THERE WERE LATE, hot September nights when Hank would roll around in bed and think about the girl who was probably named Robin, or Judith Grust, or Suzanne Smule; most of all he missed Candy Romulade and wondered why she didn't return his calls. He had liked being with her and realized that he actually worried about her; she seemed, when he thought about it, almost fragile. He tried not to watch *Perfect Fit*, and he put away the Wendy Lullabay issue of *Playboy*, but then he took it out again. Everywhere he went he noticed girls in shorts, in tight dresses. Sometimes he stared too long at strangers, thinking that he'd met them someplace before; and because Hank's Washington was a tiny place, an archipelago of neighborhoods with its small, well-off, white-skinned population, he often had. One day he saw Sam and Melanie, to whose house he'd been taken by Candy; they were approaching him along Massachusetts Avenue, carrying matching leather briefcases, and as they continued, *en passant*, there were no acknowledgments. During another lunchtime stroll, with his blazer slung over his shoulder and his beard glistening with sweat, he found himself behind another man and woman who looked familiar, and when the three of them stood at a light on Connecticut Avenue, the woman, who turned out to be Judith Grust, spoke his name.

"Hank," she said, and he thought that she looked attractive and interesting but awfully tired. There was also a lot more gray in her hair.

"Nice day," he replied, wiping his forehead.

There followed several seconds of silence while Judith was deciding whether or not to introduce Hank to her companion, someone Hank vaguely recognized. He wore a dark suit and had black shoes. His face seemed a little large—a long, thin nose and spongelike lips—and although he was probably no more than a year or two older than Hank, he seemed far more grown-up.

"Huntington Draeb," the man said, but did not offer his hand.

Hank knew the name, for he read the newspapers and had heard the stories of Draeb-inspired massacres in hot, faraway lands. He decided that he hated Huntington Draeb, which Draeb seemed to sense; he barely looked at Hank, who felt overwhelmed by Draeb's largeness, as if some exaggerated mask had been pulled over Draeb's real face. For some reason he tried to imagine Judith kissing those spongy lips, and then felt sure that she had and done perhaps more; her face had little splotches on it and her hair was not quite combed. Hank's voice quavered when he said, "You used to work for the State Department, right?" and he saw that Draeb's face got slightly darker and that his eyes almost shut, as if he were about to be angry.

"What are you saying?"

"I mean I've heard about you," Hank said, trying not to look away from the hard stare he was getting from that large, grown-up face.

Draeb raised his voice and said, "Look, I don't know who you are, but I know your type and what you're insinuating. And it makes me pretty fucking mad when people like you get all weepy and act as if you just make a choice—us or them. Well, it's not us or them; it's us, my friend."

"I'm not your friend," Hank whispered, and Judith Grust tugged at the arm of her companion; people were watching them. A bicycle messenger raced by, trailing a haze of perspiration.

"Hunt's very sensitive about this," she said, trying once more to smile at Hank.

"What do you mean by 'people like me'?" Hank said, trembling a little, and soon enough Judith was pleading with both of them to shut up.

"Either he walks away from this corner or I do," Draeb said, and Hank was off in another direction in less than five seconds. When he turned his head, he saw Draeb's arm on Judith's shoulder and wondered: wasn't she going to marry that old guy? Judith turned back too, and for a moment Hank looked at her dark, intelligent eyes and wanted to say something encouraging—to wish her good luck at the very least. Judith looked at Hank, as if she had much the same impulse, but then it was too late for that.

THIRTY-TWO

(Desperate Remedies)

Teresa Maracopulos's life had been complicated enough. Not only was her husband suspicious, but she had a feeling that he might have seen her—that it was Martin she'd glimpsed at Barkley's just before the loud disturbance that had everyone laughing. At the same time the more she saw of Reynolds Mund, the less magical he became, as when he muttered "pretty-boy shithead" if she happened to mention a network anchorman or when he called the amusing weatherman a "show-off cocksucker." She couldn't stand that he kept forgetting her name, as if he did it on purpose, and some of his habits, which she'd once thought were interesting, were turning out to be . . . *freakish*—that was the word that kept occurring to her. There was, Teresa thought, something freakish in his eagerness to talk about her husband after she'd told him how jealous and angry Martin got, or the way he liked to try on Ranger Joe's costume, or the way he'd snap his fingers and whisper "News molecule!" whenever something terrible happened to someone else, almost as if he had willed it. She'd seen him like that just the other day during *News at Six*, while the studio monitor showed pictures of a burning row house in a whitish haze. The anchorman's voice had been unnaturally low as he stared into the camera and reported that at least two children had perished—Reynolds never used "died" when he could say "perished"—and that the fate of another was unknown. A fireman coughed on camera as smoke and ash flakes swirled about, and the family's grandmother appeared; she wailed and her flimsy pajamas rippled in the bright pulse of ambulance lights. Then the anchorman had muttered those words, "news molecules," like some incantation. *Freakish.* Also he had no respect for her—the way he'd chuckled when she'd talked about being on television herself, the way he squeezed her buttocks, which was all that he'd ever tried to do. At the same time Teresa was beginning to see him in practical terms: as a very big client all her own.

. . .

MARTIN HIMMELSCHAFT recalled every detail of what he'd seen at Barkley's, in particular Teresa's intoxicated eyes and the way that her fingers had touched the anchorman's neck and rubbed his crooked nose. He thought about it at work, when he studied his pile of supervisors' reports, and at night, when he lay beside Teresa and watched *News at Eleven*. Both of them were silent as the camera went from the anchorman to the streaky-haired coanchor to the funny weatherman to the man who shouted out the sports scores. Martin knew that Teresa sensed a change in him, and yet he didn't know how to bring it up, what words to choose. He said nothing, perhaps because he feared that any answer might hurt. But suddenly Teresa's eyes had filled with tears and she said, "I know what you want to talk about, but please don't." Before Martin could reply, Teresa did something she'd not done for a while: she licked his ear. "Let me work this out," she added, in the mysterious language that she sometimes spoke.

The more that Martin thought about it in the following days, the more he blamed the place where Teresa worked and the people she associated with. He knew that he ought to watch himself—no more driving out to Candy Romulade's apartment—but one afternoon in mid-September he became so restless that he decided to visit the Big Tooth office.

The moment he showed up, people appeared to recognize this pale man whose mouth had the downward cast that mouths acquire when their owners have suffered. He wore a polo shirt that was too large and everyone watched him warily. By the time he'd made his way back to his wife's small office, Candy Romulade had prepared a stiff, sympathetic smile and stood up to kiss his cheek.

"Martin, how *are* you?" she asked.

"Fine. Where is she?" he replied.

"I'm not quite sure at this exact moment," Candy said, looking down.

"But you're always sure of everything," Martin said.

Candy, who began to scratch herself, suggested that Martin leave a note.

"Maybe I'll just stay here," he said. He sat down at Teresa's desk and tried to ignore Candy's sniff of frustration followed by a series of sighs and yawns.

Martin, feeling a little ashamed, began to examine the trove within the desk. In the center drawer he found a nearly empty tube of scarlet lipstick; a matchbook from Barkley's; a collection of rubber bands, paper clips, and lint; a self-improvement book called *Me! Me! Me!* In a narrow, deep drawer he found an unopened pair of dark panty hose, a forgotten parking ticket, a bottle of aspirin, a collection of felt-tip pens, notebooks, and a Rolodex, which had very few entries, although Martin saw that a paper clip was attached to the letter M and just behind it were three numbers for Reynolds Mund.

"Tell me about Teresa and that anchorman guy," Martin said to Candy.

"Who? Oh, you mean Reynolds?" Candy said. She plucked a cigarette from her purse and brought it to crackling life, sending gusts of gray through her nostrils. "What's there to tell?" she asked. "I'm in charge of planning his party, and Teresa is very important to the project—really important. Sort of essential."

"They seem very close, is what I mean," Martin said.

"I actually don't know what you mean," Candy said.

"I'm really asking you," Martin went on, as if picking up a recent argument, "to tell me what you won't tell me."

"Your thing is falling off," Candy said, and pointed to the alligator dangling by a thread from his shirt.

"I'd better find that guy myself," Martin said, standing up. "Maybe talk to him."

"Please don't do anything to ruin things for all of us," Candy said, but Martin wasn't listening. Rather he was picking up Teresa's coffee mug, which he examined briefly before throwing it as hard as he could at a wall, frightening a man with a red face and a worried look who was on his way to see Candy.

.   .   .

"What the hell was that?" Charlie Dingleman wondered when he saw the furious man who'd just smashed a coffee mug. He knew that he looked a little battered himself; he'd noticed white hairs floating toward his shoes the last time he'd gone for a haircut, not quite believing that those feathery tufts were his, and he'd lost so much weight that his clothes—even his shoes—were roomier. He guessed that Candy pitied him, which was embarrassing, yet he knew that her pity might be helpful. All in all Charlie had never felt quite so sorry for himself; he'd even begun to get a dull pain in an upper-right molar—just a bit sensitive when he brushed, but a little more sensitive each day. Dentists wanted money too; everyone did, and the money was running low. Then there was Eve's letter, which eventually got to the point about a divorce and selling the R Street house but began by announcing a liaison with some Englishman named Ian: "His family," she wrote, "has the most beautiful place in England, in Sussex or Essex, which is where I want to live when we retire and our children are grown. You must be thinking about that too by now—I mean retirement. Also, Ian is very interested in learning about politics, so he'd really enjoy meeting you."

Charlie wondered when this Ian had actually entered the picture, and he thought about Eve's long, curved nose, her tiny panties, and her conspiratorial whispers. He thought about James too but tried not to think. "I won't stay long," he said to Candy.

. . .

CANDY WAS SHOCKED by Charlie Dingleman's aspect, although she could not have said what precisely had been altered. She wondered if he'd been sick and she noticed the dime-sized grease spot on his tie and the stubble sprouts where his razor had missed. She tried to pay attention to what he was saying, but it sounded unbelievably silly. The poor man wanted to pee on his own front lawn, and so what? Who on earth would care about that? She wished that Charlie wasn't quite so emotional; the poor guy looked about ready to cry. She didn't have time for this; with all she had to do for the Reynolds Mund gala, she sometimes felt that she was going crazy. She was furious at Teresa for being at the television studio when her crazy husband showed up, and on a very different subject, she thought that she ought to disinvite Hank Morriday, whom she'd thought she could count on, who'd behaved so ridiculously and un-helpfully the last time. And then Hank had done something unbe-lievable: he'd just written an unbelievable article for the newspaper explaining why someone like him was going to vote for someone like George Bush. Candy just wished that Charlie would leave—he hadn't even paid his bill—and yet she wanted to help. "Like I said," she said, "maybe Teresa can talk to Reynolds."

A moment later Candy's telephone buzzed so loudly that Charlie nearly jumped: it was Dennis, who needed to speak to Teresa about the Mund gala. "I'll try to find her, Mr. Secretary," Candy said, and then she lit a cigarette and inhaled as if every breath could save her life. She wished that Charlie weren't looking at her so pitifully, like a needy dog, and then she patted his hand as if it were a paw.

THIRTY-THREE

MAYBE IT WAS Candy Romulade's influence, but Hank Morriday had also been thinking of abandoning the life that he'd been leading: his peeling building in Adams Morgan on its seedy block with its smells of invisible tortillas; his apartment with its pile of unread magazines, so heavy with the dust of information that he could not bear to toss them out. He thought of teaching in a college town with bright steeples and pretty girls. Or he might change careers, learn the tricks of Wall Street that were making others so rich. (His college roommate had made shrewd investments in fiber optics.) Or he could "get down in the trenches," as they said to one another at the Institute, which had come to mean almost anything resembling actual work. He reflected with mild despair about his incomplete manuscript, about being shunned by colleagues, and about the near absence of a personal life. It was all this, Hank later thought, along with the torment of the presidential election, which actually got him to write his notorious column. Hank knew that others questioned his motives, doubted his sincerity, and yet he saw his words as a brave departure from his past—one that made total sense, considering his present.

Candy at least had not totally shunned him, and he was pleased when she called to remind him about the Reynolds Mund gala, which he knew would be a major Washington event. He wondered why Candy hadn't said anything about his essay, and he hoped for

another night with her, one that ended in her condo with her legs
wrapped tight around his hips. By the evening of the party Hank
was thinking about Candy with both longing and affection; as he
shook dust from his cummerbund and searched for matching cuff
links, he looked forward to all of it; and as he climbed into his
BMW, dust and rain streaking the green finish, he thought that the
city had never looked as magical as it did in this autumn of 1988.

He took a roundabout way to Barkley's, stopping at the Tidal
Basin to lean against the railing and stare into the black water,
where he spotted bits of trash and, he imagined, the eyes of fish.
The leather seats, the bursts of jazz coming from the speakers as he
gripped the knob of the gearshift, delighted him. Hank took it as a
good omen that he found a parking spot on L Street, and when he
showed up at Barkley's, he saw that the restaurant had been made
over. The wax John Foster Dulles clutched an invitation in its hand,
banners were strung on the walls, each one saying "All Our Yester-
days, All Our Tomorrows. He'll Always Surprise You," and in the
main dining room, where the tables had been pushed to the walls,
Reynolds Mund's face filled several television screens. Anyone who
did more than glance at these screens would notice that great care
had been taken with chronology so that one saw the anchorman in
1968, his sideburns long and dark as he sidled up to a beleaguered
Hubert Humphrey, and then saw that face, its warm smile intact,
changing in the twenty years (and through all the astonishing hap-
penings) that led to this evening. Only a diligent student of his career would have spotted the late arrival of hairs along his crooked
nose and a more frequent blankness in his eyes.

When Hank got there, the room was almost empty, and he
looked around, trying to see if he knew any of the early arrivals
along the periphery. As he tugged at his cummerbund, he watched
for food, and finding none he headed to the bar, where he asked for
white wine. He sipped this too-sweet liquid as he looked for Candy,

knowing that she would be among the first on the scene; then while checking his reflection, he felt his left hand being squeezed by a chubby man with a green incisor. It took him a moment to recognize freckled, red-haired Joachim, the Austrian diplomat who had never gone back to Vienna.

"It is so good to meet again!" declared the Austrian, who wore an English suit and whose skin had turned, it appeared, orange. "Where have you been keeping yourself, my good fellow?" This question seemed more a demand than a query, but before Hank could answer, Joachim turned, searching the room until he saw another face that Hank had nearly forgotten. "Gretel!" he called out. "Look who's here!"

Hank sipped his wine and tried to smile. He was not eager to speak to Joachim and Gretel, but so far they were the only people who recognized him. He saw passing by a tall yellow-haired woman who looked like a model, her pale blue dress slipping from one shoulder to the other, her shadowed eyes not seeing Hank.

"Such a pity about poor Mr. Dukakis," Joachim said when Gretel was beside him and nodding agreement. "It seems likely now, according to your polls, that he will lose, eh? What a shame!"

The two Austrians looked dolorous yet almost gleeful. Hank realized that they probably thought, as they had before, that he was not himself but his doppelganger, Crane.

"You know, the thing is that I have faith in the judgment of the American people," Hank said, and he thought about his column and added, "lots of faith."

Joachim gave him a confidential chuckle.

"We also think not too badly of George Bush and Mr. Quayle. We have so many friends here. We love Washington!"

Hank did not hear these last words because he'd just spotted the woman whose name, he believed, was Robin. He thought that her skin had never seemed so smooth, her eyes so wide and searching. He imagined her unclothed; it was unbearable.

A battalion of perspiring waiters in white coats soared by them, and as Hank reached out, a cheeselike hors d'oeuvre fell to the floor and was crushed by one of Joachim's shiny shoes. Hank saw that Barkley's was far more crowded than it had been just ten minutes before. The sound of conversation was louder, and now and then, like an instrument's solo, a giddy laugh, soprano or bass, would sweep through. At the bar an apprehensive Salvadoran poured drinks and wiped his forehead with a white towel. Hank noticed a chalky-faced man with dark patches under his eyes, someone he'd seen before, as he had seen so many others, but could not recall where. And where was Candy? He supposed that she was with the guest of honor, who hadn't arrived either. He found himself at Robin's side, surprised that she offered him her pink cheek, which he kissed, but displeased that she moved away so swiftly when she recognized him.

The room was quite suddenly crammed with people and considerably warmer from the accumulation of bodies, most of them now clutching drinks and food morsels. Hank to his relief was seeing more people that he recognized. He was so glad that he'd come. Over by the window was a Cabinet secretary, and by his side was the columnist Brandon Sladder chatting with the Iraqi ambassador, and there was Suzanne Smule, wearing a dark blue taffeta dress and pearl necklace. Hank walked her way, hoping for more than that apprehensive look she was giving him.

"I've been worrying that perestroika is not working," he said when he caught up with her, bending to kiss her cheek before she could dodge him, his beard evidently tickling her.

"I'm very surprised to see you here," she said. "I can't believe you wrote that."

"That's what Sakharov was saying anyway," he persisted, paying no attention to what Suzanne Smule had just said.

She stepped away from him, stopped by another white-coated waiter weaving through the darkly dressed crowd, and then she fled. Hank hoped that no one had seen that exchange, and when he turned around, Joachim the Austrian was there again, telling him there was someone he wanted Hank to meet. They had, of course, met before.

"A member of our diplomatic fraternity," Joachim said beaming, and Hank nodded to the guileful-faced author of *My Four Trouble Spots*, which had become a best-seller in Washington. "He's one of my very favorite people in our little village," the Austrian said.

When the former diplomat extended his hand, Hank thought it strange that it was the left one.

"My publisher has begged me for more—for a 'last spot,' so to speak," the author said. "My first thought was something the French prime minister once observed at a dinner party—how the last spot always ends on your pants. And that will be my title!" The memoirist chuckled and dashed off, having spied someone else.

. . .

IN A LITTLE WHILE Hank saw that just about all of Washington was there, and he walked around the restaurant several times to be sure everyone saw that he was there too. There were rumors that Reagan himself might drop by (a few watchful strangers with earplugs stood near the exits) or someone who had earned the right to a cadre of security. In his rounds Hank saw Pete Thingeld, a founding partner of one of the city's oldest and most powerful law firms, dandruff covering the shoulders of his tuxedo, talking to Judith Grust's fiancé, that sad-looking elderly man with a bruised lip, and Judith herself, looking uncomfortable—another cheek to kiss.

"Hank's an old friend and an expert on welfare," Judith said. When Hank began to explain the enormity of the problem, the despair of the unskilled, and the need for early childhood intervention, they acted as if they couldn't quite hear him.

"You two getting married?" Hank asked, turning from Judith to Alfred Schmalz and back again, and the hot black warning that Hank saw in her eyes unnerved him.

"It's under discussion," Schmalz said, his bruised lip barely moving, and he appeared to glare at Judith, all of this driving Hank to head elsewhere: he had spotted Randolph Maintree, and he tried to catch the eye of the director of the Institute, who managed not to see him, even when Hank passed right by.

There was a rush to one side of the room when the shrimp and oysters were unveiled, and dozens of men and women came away with red sauce dripping from their teeth, and then a rush to the other when the sushi went on display. Hank felt a heavy lump in his stomach from the hors d'oeuvres he'd already socked away, and all the while he looked around for the missing anchorman and Candy Romulade. He saw a former astronaut with a gold Big Tooth lapel pin and wild eyes talking to a short, slightly plump woman, and Hank recognized her as the one who shared Candy's office—Teresa something-or-other. Her dress was low and her large breasts were half visible; he tried not to stare at them or at the two silver teeth between them.

Not everyone seemed to belong. The man with the pale face, the one Hank thought he'd seen before, looked nervously uneasy, but everyone knew that the anchorman had accumulated a wide circle of friends in his two decades on the air. There came a moment when the crowd seemed to fill every inch of Barkley's. Hank gave a small, possibly desperate wave (wanting to retrieve it) toward Randolph Maintree, which was intercepted (and not returned) by the tall woman in the pale blue dress. The people standing next to Hank were talking about the election—Bush, Dukakis, how many states each would win, the polls in California and the South—and no one really seemed to care that Reynolds Mund had not yet shown up for his own party. Hank caught sight of Huntington Draeb, his nose like a sharp crease down the center of his face; when he lighted a skinny cigar, it was as if the line extended outward to a provocative, fiery tip, and Draeb went to stand next to Pete Thingeld, Judith Grust, and Alfred Schmalz, all of whom looked uncomfortable in one another's presence.

The pale-faced man was heading his way, and Hank found himself shaking hands with Martin Himmelschaft. The man shrugged and said, "I don't know anybody here, but I've seen you someplace."

"I've seen you too," Hank replied, and then remembered how this man had shown up one evening outside Candy's building. Hank looked self-consciously around, not wanting to stand here with this out-of-place man he did not know. "We could be watching the play-offs," the man said, as Hank moved away and with a congenial nod replied, "Yeah." The Hank Morriday whose influential thoughts on race and poverty and now politics had been published in journals of opinion and who dated—and had actual sexual intercourse with—serious women like Judith Grust and Candy Romulade should not, he thought, devote time, not even seconds, to people like this. People judged others by how they dressed and the company they kept, and Hank was embarrassed at the thought of being seen with this man by people like Suzanne Smule and Randolph Maintree and no doubt dozens of others.

·   ·   ·

WHEN HANK SAW Candy Romulade, her tawny bare back was facing him and she appeared to be whispering excitedly to Huntington Draeb. "I was reading up on you," Candy was telling Hunt, speaking rapidly, her lined face anxious. "I was thinking how I want to see you involved with some humanitarian cause. It would be very good for you at this point in your career, believe me. There are a number of other options we should explore, but I

think that's the key. Maybe a Third World country you've never been involved with?"

Robin pushed by Hank, followed by the Jesuit who couldn't stop talking about women and the woman in the pale blue dress, whose buttocks grazed Hank's hand, and dozens of others as the crowd parted. This happened because the honored guest, the anchorman himself, had arrived. As he strode through the crowd and smiled his crinkly smile, a spotlight found him, as did the hot lights of camera crews; the guests, all of them far too warm, applauded.

The anchorman looked, Hank thought, a little wobbly, but no less reassuring with his crooked, hairy nose and warm grin and kindly eyes. He was accompanied only by Candy and Teresa. As the applause got louder, Hank felt himself drifting away from the clatter of this familiar place. When someone tugged at his wrist, a signal to get out of the way, he stood on his toes to keep up with the warm, blinking stare of the sweat-soaked anchorman, who now took over all the television screens that had, for several minutes, been flickering and empty.

When the celebrant spoke in his trademark raspy voice, he told his friends and admirers that he owed everything to a discovery he'd made a few years before. "I'm no scientist," he said, "but I've gotten to where I am because I've learned how to make news molecules," and at that almost everyone fell silent. Then they saw his warm grin and their applause started up again. "Believe me," the anchorman went on, "there will be plenty more where those came from. Just watch," he added as he reached out to embrace a woman nearby, the one with the silver teeth between her large breasts. The guests, a little puzzled, clapped, or most of them did, from the most powerful people in Washington to two policemen named Louis and Quella. One exception was an unhealthy-looking administrator from the personnel office of the District government whom almost no one had seen before. Pushed by the crowd, the bureaucrat bent down to pick up a piece of discarded camera equipment. Hank Morriday clapped too, but he felt odd as he looked around, looking everywhere, as if he might get a glimpse of someone else he knew, perhaps someone from his past, and he thought unexpectedly of his very first days in Washington, how pastoral and pretty and exciting it had been, and of a Smith girl with a ponytail whom he'd tried to date twenty years ago, or of anyone closer to him than these people with their tidbits of food and drink and opinion. He supposed that after a while, after a few more years like this, only tidbits of his own life would remain and that it wouldn't matter very much what he did.

Hank was having these thoughts when he saw the pale-faced man approaching the guest of honor, who was trying now to kiss the short, pretty woman who wore the silver teeth. The short woman screamed when she saw that her husband bore a metal tripod, which in his hands looked threatening. She screamed louder and cried out something that sounded like "Oh shit!" when the angry man, for whom the only person there who mattered was his sweetheart, tried to bring that three-legged implement down upon the wavy hair of the legendary local anchorman, who dove to the floor, out of the way, chuckling; and when the furious man tried again, he stumbled and fell next to the anchorman. The short, pretty woman, still screaming and possibly weeping, wrapped her arms around them both. Others in the room yelled too, for it was the sort of moment that encouraged such behavior, and the lights seemed to shine brighter as the volume increased and the policemen, Louis and Quella, pushed toward the front, although a little sleepily. Soon enough there were sirens: the stranger was hauled away, everyone left had something to talk about, and the anchorman smiled and mumbled something that only a few people close by were sure they understood.

THIRTY-FOUR

A FEW DAYS AFTER the anchorman's big party, Candy Romulade was fired. "You have to understand, Candy, that we're basically happy with your performance," Dennis said, tapping his tightly curled blond hair with the tips of his fingers. "But here's the problem: you're not bringing in clients, which is our life's blood."

"No, but I mean I try, Mr. Secretary," Candy replied, knowing that was the wrong answer. "Also I thought the party was a big success," another wrong answer.

Dennis nodded and then said, "From what I understand, Mr. Mund was not happy with his party."

"Not happy?" Candy asked. "How come?"

Dennis looked at a sheet of paper and studied it while he shook his head and licked his lips.

"He was upset because no one from the network was there to honor him and because nothing was in the newspaper," Dennis said in a firm mumble. "He felt that no one noticed—which is the same thing as having no party at all. He blamed us and he was right to blame us."

Dennis rubbed his head.

"I invited those people," Candy said, although she had left that part up to Teresa and—*idiot!*—it might have slipped by her. "I can't force anyone to show up."

"Also people he didn't like showed up," Dennis said, and added,

"Especially that weird guy who could have really hurt him." He paused and added, "You seemed to know that weird guy."

Candy did not know how to reply—no one, including Teresa, seemed to want to know who Martin was—but before she could try, Dennis went on, "As I told you, it's not about one event; it's about earning your keep. We're in a recession or something." He shrugged. "I don't know."

It was true that business had been slow; Candy was well aware that several important clients had become fugitives. But she had hoped to do her part; she mentioned Huntington Draeb and the author of *My Four Trouble Spots* as people she'd had her eye on. But when Dennis's eyes went out of focus, it all began to seem too much, and she thought about the joshing Asian colonel, the one who was rumored to swallow the ears of his enemies, who'd come in and hugged everyone, including Candy, whose ear he'd nibbled playfully, and about Hank Morriday, whom she'd ignored, having more or less decided that Hank was not the man for her. So while she started to protest her dismissal—"Dennis, this really isn't fair"—she felt a simultaneous giddy cheeriness. She imagined how it would feel to do something else, almost anything else, and for that moment felt as if she were aloft, floating all the way to Minnesota. "I really don't understand how you can smile," Dennis said.

The first person Candy told was Teresa Maracopulos, who said that she couldn't believe it. "If you're not here, I don't want to stay," Teresa said. But as she hugged the best work friend she'd ever had, Teresa understood that she hadn't meant a word of it and that in some way this might actually be good for her. She was ashamed of having that thought, but she couldn't make it disappear, especially later that day when Dennis smiled at her and hinted at a better Big Tooth future. Teresa was particularly ashamed of pretending not to know who Martin was.

"Are you insane?" she had said to Martin on the night of the party, long after midnight, when the police had let him go. "This could be really bad for me at the office."

He'd kept apologizing, but within a week Teresa decided that just as Big Tooth had fired Candy, she was going to have to fire Martin. She found a one-bedroom apartment near Dupont Circle, close enough to walk to work, and left a deposit with the landlord, a bony man with popping blue eyes. She couldn't believe that it was just a month before another Thanksgiving with her family.

. . .

ON THE MORNING that Candy threw out the accumulation of several years (broken sunglasses, Carter-Mondale buttons, pink telephone messages, a small hair dryer, business cards from the Federal Trade Commission), she had one chore left; as Charlie Dingleman had put it, "Candy, you've got to save my bacon," which made her think of rescuing burnt strips from puddles of hot grease.

Until now every time Candy had brought it up, Teresa had looked at her helplessly. "He won't listen," she'd said. "He'll hate me for asking." But this time Teresa shrugged and said she'd try if Candy came along; after all Candy had been her very best work friend, and maybe it wasn't so much to ask.

Before they left, Candy and Teresa drank a glass a wine and then another. They got to the television station just before Reynolds went off the air, and because everyone knew Teresa, they were immediately let into the small newsroom. From a corner they watched the robot cameras as the weatherman did a tap dance and the long-haired coanchor stretched her lips and the sports reporter giggled. As soon as *News at Five* was done, everyone rushed away from the scruffy set.

"Hello, my lovelies," the anchorman said in his raspy voice when he saw Candy and Teresa.

"We need to talk to you," Candy said.

"Uh-oh, that sounds serious," he replied, and frowned seriously.

"Come along then," he said, and they followed him to his private office. A solemn portrait of Walter Cronkite hung on a wall; on his desk a pair of silvery spurs leaned against a large white cowboy hat. He sat between Candy and Teresa on a purple leather sofa.

"Oh, that's a sad story," the anchorman said with a melancholy smile when Candy made her request. "Very, very sad," he added, then muttered excitedly, "Newsmolecule," as if it were one word.

He patted one of Teresa's thighs, a long finger rubbing. His hand, as it rested there, felt very cold.

"But it's not a true story," Candy said. "And I know that you're a very fair person; that's why Washington loves you." Candy was pleased with her approach and tried her most seductive smile. When the anchorman didn't respond, she asked, perhaps a little more sharply than she'd meant to, "Did you hear what I just said?"

"I ignored it purposely," he replied.

He began to hum and then to sing the words to the Ranger Joe song. "'For Ranger Joe, it's time to go, but let's be partners again,'" he sang, and by the second chorus Candy wondered why no one told him to get rid of the quivering hairs that sprang up like spines from his crooked nose.

"You know," the anchorman said, "that song is really about my partnership with this town. We're very close."

"I would really appreciate it if you'd listen," Candy said, tapping her fingers as Teresa looked uncomfortable.

"I always listen," the anchorman replied, turning toward Candy and resting his other cold hand on her knee. His nose twitched, and looking amused, he smiled.

"I know you do; that's why you're so good at what you do," Candy said, and lit a cigarette. "But this story is all wrong," she went on, and was about to say more when the anchorman suddenly stood up. He took Ranger Joe's ten-gallon hat and smacked it against the desk. The sound of felt hitting wood was as loud as a gunshot.

"Stop that," the anchorman said, his friendly grin gone and his eyes nearly shut. "You seem to have no *idea* what I do. My producer told me it was a very good story. He is going to the *White House!*"

"It's a very bad story," Candy said in a whisper, proud of her professionalism and wishing that Charlie or Dennis or someone could see her in action. "I'm talking about *ruining* that poor man's life for no good reason."

"I'm told that his penis was in full view," the anchorman replied, his voice gentler, more patient. "We have the police report; it's all there, honey. It's a very good combination: White House and penis." He shook his head and smiled and muttered, "Newsmolecule!"

In Candy's mind Charlie Dingleman was clinging by his fingertips to a tall building. "He was just, like, peeing in his front yard," she said. "I can't believe a big man like you cares about a little thing like that."

The anchorman's eyes got foggier, his face seemed to tremble, and then he turned away. For several minutes Candy and Teresa watched while he went through letters and newspaper clippings and telephone messages. He rattled the silver spurs.

"I'm sorry," Teresa said, speaking for the first time, hating this discussion or whatever it was. "I don't always understand what you do."

"No, you don't," he replied. "How could you? I know that you worship me."

"I don't worship you," Teresa said, her expression miserable and defiant. "We should go," she said to Candy.

"Don't go, Tabitha," the anchorman said, and rested his head on his hands. After a while he looked up and said, "No one's ever heard of him anyway," and at first Candy and Teresa did not realize what he'd said. When they did, Teresa went to his side and stroked his nose and patted his hair. "Teresa," she said, and it actually took her several days to realize that this had been a farewell pat, that she was firing Reynolds Mund too, although certainly not as a client.

Before they left, the anchorman pointed to a recent newspaper column by a man he'd once interviewed, a social theorist, someone named Hank Morriday. It was the column, already widely discussed in Washington, where this Morriday fellow explained why, although he was a lifelong Democrat, he had decided to vote for Bush over Dukakis. "An interesting guy," the anchorman observed.

"If you'd like to interview him," Candy said, putting out her cigarette, "I can definitely arrange it."

THIRTY-FIVE

Hank Morriday had written his little essay (published under the title "Why I Switched") in the middle of the night, now and then opening the Wendy Lullabay issue of *Playboy* as he pushed on, writing, he later told someone, "in a fever pitch." He was flattered by the attention it brought him, such as the rebuttal by Crane and Suzanne Smule, "Why We're Loyal." What he didn't appreciate was the personal stuff, like the way he'd been snubbed at the party for Reynolds Mund and also at the Institute, where someone had crammed another note into his mail slot, this one saying "SCUM-BAG!" In the elevator Randolph Maintree had said, "You're amazing, Morriday," then had fallen silent when Hank attempted to pursue that thought. After that no one there spoke to him at all.

Among the people he heard from was Judith Grust, although she didn't mention the column; rather she left a message saying that it was nice to have run into him at the anchorman's party and wasn't it dreadful that they'd fallen so out of touch? Also there was something important that they ought to discuss. Candy Romulade called too, but she just wanted to help set up a television interview; she hadn't seemed to appreciate his writing. Also she wanted to tell him that Big Tooth had fired her. "Hey, I know what you're going through," Hank said, and asked her to have dinner with him. But she was mysteriously busy.

In early November Candy called once more to ask—hypothetically of course—if Hank would consider working with one of her old clients, a fairly conservative Republican, although someone, she was sure, who would approve of "the Morriday philosophy."

"I'm open to new ideas, as you know," Hank replied.

"When I was going through my old stuff, I thought of you," Candy said, as Hank thought about her wounded smile and felt himself receding into her past. "This person I'm referring to knows that you care about people," Candy continued, and Hank assured her that to him no species on earth mattered more.

"Who is it?" he asked, wishing there was a way to close the distance that had come between them. It was as if he were talking to someone he'd never met. "Someone with Bush?" he added hopefully.

"As you know, I tried to broaden my client base when I was there," Candy said, "and I can see that you've been doing the same." She paused for such a long time that Hank wondered if she'd hung up. Then she added, "He's a compassionate guy who's been through a lot. I think you could help each other."

"I don't know," Hank said.

"Just thought I'd ask," Candy said.

"I'd like to meet him," Hank said. "And I'd love to see you too, Candy," he added, not for the first time.

"That's going to be more difficult," she replied.

. . .

UNLIKE DUKAKIS, with whom he'd never become very close (as he put it), Hank felt comfortable right away with this middle-aged man, although he seemed a little despairing, almost to the point of suffering, when they met in the living room of his curiously empty Georgetown house. Hank at one point admired the sculpture in a corner, the one that seemed to represent various limbs of a small dead tree, but his host did not acknowledge the compliment; rather he kept staring at a dented telephone, as if waiting for a call.

At first conversation was difficult, especially on Hank's side when he thought about the part, the minuscule part, he had played in trying to wreck this particular person's life, but also when he had to listen to Charlie Dingleman's ideas about helping the poor and the untrained. Nevertheless when Charlie said, "Put the lazy bastards to work is my thought, and you'll solve a lot of problems," Hank was not as troubled as he might have been a few months earlier; in fact he realized that he felt a sort of primal agreement.

Charlie showed Hank newspaper clippings about his last campaign, which described how Charlie sometimes looked pleadingly into the eyes of voters, a technique that observant reporters everywhere described as a "rare glimpse of raw emotion." Hank for his part praised Candy Romulade and showed Charlie "Why I Switched," which, it turned out, Charlie had not read or even heard about. Hank tugged at his beard and felt a new wave of embarrassment over what he'd once done to this friendly guy—well, not quite done; after all, Charlie had done it to himself. Hank noticed a quivering cobweb in a corner of the ceiling, glistening with lost light.

A day or so before the election Hank looked up from his desk at the Institute to see Judith Grust materialize by his half-opened door; right away he got up and gripped her arms and kissed her cheek. When he stood back, he thought that she had become remarkably thinner in a very short time and that weariness enveloped her.

"You look wonderful," Hank said.

"So do you," Judith replied. She closed her eyes and seemed to stall on the incline of her next words. "You didn't call back, but some things are better said in person."

"You sound so serious," Hank said. "Did you like my article?"

Judith stared at Hank with her thoughtful eyes.

"What article?" she asked. "I wanted to tell you about me—that I'm a partner now. Maybe you knew that? Also that I was going to marry someone in the firm. Maybe you knew that too?" She closed her eyes, as if she were meditating. "Or I thought I was."

"The old man?" Hank said, a little sorry at the way the words came out because he felt, as they spoke, a stirring for Judith. "I thought you might have something going with that Draeb guy," he added, and the look on her face told him that he'd said too much already.

"I'm having a difficult time making choices," Judith said, biting a lip.

She looked around for a chair and, finding none, sat on the corner of Hank's desk, placing one knee a few inches from his face. She reached for a thick ballpoint pen on the desk and began to roll it in her hands. Hank watched her thin, powerful wrists at work and thought how smooth her knee looked under her dark stockings.

"Are you okay?" Judith asked with creamy solicitude. "To tell you the truth, you didn't seem completely right in the head that night at that party."

Hank studied her knee. He pulled at his beard and made himself smile, although he couldn't sustain it. "I have something to tell you too," he said, and he told Judith about Charlie Dingleman. Judith broke the ballpoint pen in half.

"I can't believe you're involved with him in any way," she said, and then said it again.

"He was happy to meet me," Hank said, scratching a temple. "He appreciates my ideas, and you know what?" he continued a little angrily. "I *like* that." Hank managed another smile and chose his words carefully, wanting to explain that he was, in a broad sense, shifting alliances. "I could be a domestic honcho," he finished up. He had never used the word "honcho" before.

"I don't want to argue with you, Hank," Judith said, her voice softer. "But I can't believe you've forgotten what you did to him."

"What *we* did—what *you* wanted," Hank replied, but his smile, as if caught in the fringes of his beard, wilted.

For several seconds Judith stared at Hank as if he were a key witness and she were about to pounce. Then she said, "I won't tell if you won't."

"Okay," Hank said, half-sighing, feeling light with relief when there was no pounce, absently squeezing her knee. She glanced at his hand and was about to say something. Then she brushed it away.

"Someone once said that lies are the lubricant of civilization," she said, sliding off the desk. "I'm pretty sure that's the truth."

"Me too," Hank said, not quite listening, and then his telephone rang. He wondered who could be calling: Charlie Dingleman, perhaps, or Reynolds Mund, who seemed really interested in his ideas, or maybe even the White House. Hank flapped his fingers—a good-bye to Judith—and supposed, almost happily, that from now on anything was possible.

ACKNOWLEDGMENTS

HEARTFELT THANKS to Geoffrey Kloske, Tina Bennett, David Remnick, Henry Finder, and my beloved Diana for their encouragement and intellectual generosity.

ABOUT THE AUTHOR

JEFFREY FRANK is a senior editor at *The New Yorker* and is the author of *The Columnist*. He lives in Manhattan with his wife, Diana.